THE BEAUTIFUL INDIFFERENCE

Sarah Hall was born in Cumbria in 1974. She is the author of four novels, *Haweswater*, *The Electric Michelangelo*, *The Carhullan Army* and *How to Paint a Dead Man*, and the winner of, amongst others, the Commonwealth Writers' Prize, the Betty Trask Award, the John Llewellyn Rhys Prize and the Portico Prize for Fiction. *The Electric Michelangelo* was also shortlisted for the Man Booker Prize and longlisted for the Orange Prize for Fiction.

Further praise for *The Beautiful Indifference*:

'Seven skilfully adrenalised stories, precise and sensual, in which the scent of violence is a constant.' Helen Simpson, *Guardian* Books of the Year

'I love the lyricism in these darkly erotic stories, the stark beauty of Hall's prose, its quiet precision. Individually stunning, together these tales comprise a tour-de-force collection that has reignited my love of the short story.' S. J. Watson

'Hall evokes her landscapes with bewitchingly vivid prose. Her writing is guttural and visceral, and her characters are raw and sinewy . . . Every one of the seven tales here delights and disturbs in equal measure. *The Beautiful Indifference* illustrates that short fiction is indeed a finely wrought art form, and Hall is an artist of considerable and concise skill.' *Sunday Times*

'There is an air of quiet desolation about the stories, and an understated storytelling nous, like Alice Munro or Raymond Carver, yet with a distinct personality all her own. Measured, discomforting and occasionally sublime, it's a fine addition to her body of work.' *Big Issue*

'This varied and engrossing selection . . . shows Hall's brilliant gift for character and the sensuous drama of her writing.' *Psychologies*

'[Hall] creates some glorious imagery . . . the reader's memory still lingers on a beautifully realised moment or skilfully drawn character.' *The List*

'Luscious short stories from uber-talented Cumbrian writer Sarah Hall, all told in ravishing prose.' *Metro*

'Details are what life is about, and Hall registers them masterfully.' *TLS*

'Hall's vaunted writing prowess is apparent

throughout. She evokes location skilfully and sensuously, whether an eerie Finnish lake without apparent bottom, a moneyed, conservative city coming apart at the seams on a drunken Saturday night, or desolate Cumbrian fells where the stench of the local abattoir drifts across valleys steeped in centuries of warfare . . . Without judgement, Hall seems to set her characters, and by extension all of us, on a scale with animals, rutting by instinct, violent at heart, governed by the same needs for warmth, sex, shelter and food.' *Daily Telegraph*

'Hall masters landscape and brevity both, sending you places mentally as well as emotionally then hauling you elsewhere . . . Hall's stories are disturbing and delicate, surprising and sad, assured and sensual, with a deliciously dark tint to their edges. What better recommendation for a book of short stories than to be so enchanted that you want to flip them over and start all over again.' *Scotland on Sunday*

by the same author

Haweswater
The Electric Michelangelo
The Carhullan Army
How to Paint a Dead Man

The Beautiful Indifference

SARAH HALL

faber and faber

First published in 2011
by Faber and Faber Limited
Bloomsbury House
74–77 Great Russell Street
London WC1B 3DA

This paperback edition first published in 2012

Typeset by Faber and Faber Ltd
Printed and bound by CPI Group (UK) Ltd, Croydon CR0 4YY

'Butcher's Perfume' was shortlisted for the BBC National Short Story Award
2010. The story was published by Comma Press and recorded by BBC
Radio 4 in association with the Award in 2010. 'Bees' was first published in
Underwords: The Hidden City by Maia Press in 2005. 'She Murdered Mortal
He' was first published in the October 2011 edition of *Granta*. 'The
Nightlong River' was first published under the title 'Mink' by www.pulp.net
in 2006. 'Vuotjärvi' was long-listed for the Sunday Times EFG Private Bank
Short Story Award 2011 and was first published in 2011 as an ebook by
Fast Fiction for Kindle.

'Speirin' from *The Tree House* by Kathleen Jamie reproduced by permission
of Pan Macmillan, London. Copyright © Kathleen Jamie, 2004

A CIP record for this book
is available from the British Library

ISBN 978-0-571-23018-1

2 4 6 8 10 9 7 5 3 1

For James

Contents

Binna feart, hinny,
yin day we'll gang thegither
tae thae stourie
blaebellwids,
and loss wirsels –

see, I'd raither
whummel a single oor
intae the blae o thae wee flo'ers
than live fur a' eternity
in some cauld hivvin.

from 'Speirin' by Kathleen Jamie

Butcher's Perfume

Later, when I knew her better, Manda told me how she'd beaten two girls at once outside the Cranemakers Arms in Carlisle. She said all you had to do was keep hold of one, keep hold of one and keep hitting her. No matter what the other was doing to you, you kept that first one pinned, and you kept hammering her, so the free-handed bitch could see you were able to take a flailing and still have her mate at the same time. It'd get into the lass's head then, Manda said, what it would be like when the mate got put down, and you went to batter her next without a silly dog on your back making you slow. Chances were you wouldn't have to fight them both. And if you did, that second one would be so fleart from you being still upright after her best, undefended go, she'd forget any moves she knew.

Manda was fiercer than all of us. It had nothing to do with her size – it never does with girls, for the willowy tall ones are often gentle as you like. Manda was small – maybe five foot two. She wasn't squat either, not pelvic, or thick with glands and brawn. It was in her eyes. She had eyes that got set off easily, like a dog chained up all its life and kicked about, prone to attack for no other provocation than it catches you looking its way. All you can do is pray the chain holds at the stake. And it was in her brain. She didn't have a switch in there that stopped her from pulling back her fist, like the rest of us. That's why we were all afraid of her. That's why her name went before her – Manda Slessor – and if you heard it said in a room you felt ill at ease, you felt things shift out of the way for its coming into the conversation. Everyone knew she was hard. It was the first thing ever they knew about her. It was her pedigree.

People said she was raised to it, with that family of hers. There was a lot of arrogance and expectation mixed up in the Slessors. They were known for prison sentences, and pig-iron money that built them a big house above the town's industrial estate. They had reputations for fertility at every age, for a seed that always took, and a womb that always produced – thirteen and virgin to those traveller grandmothers suckling at fifty. The town thought it understood their cause – they'd been forged from the old rage of the north, it was said. They were not drovers or farmers, nor the quiet settlers of the Borders. They came from gipsy stock, scrappies, dog- and horse-breeders, fire-mongers.

These were the ones who lit the beacons when other folk hid in cellars and down wells. They smeared offal on their chests and waited at the citadel with their bearded hounds for the Scots. These were the ones who took trophy heads and played football with them in the streets. They had Pictish hearts that allied with an enemy for the sake of avoiding slaughter, but never forgot the original blood of their tribe. And a generation on, at the turning of the Solway tide, there would be a reckoning. The men would take up arms. The women would braid boars' hair into their own. They'd murder their infants birthed to the offcoming sires. Where does history end, we were once asked in school.

With the Muslims, some clever-arse shouted.

You may as well ask where true north begins.

The father, Geordie Slessor, went about town like the next in line for the throne, beating the Duke of Edinburgh every year at the local horse-driving trials with a trap team of Heltondale Fells reared from his own entires. Come June you'd see him practising along the roads, green-Barboured, leaning back from the reins. He was gristle right through to the bone. The brothers were fighters too, the three of them, and they all had the same eyes as Manda, got from their gipsy mam: healthy blue, polished up to a high gleam, and set against bad skin. Manda was the sole daughter and she had her own tough clave quality that went beyond family; something not inherited, something made perfectly for hitting off another surface. You'll think me a daft mare for saying that. But sometimes there's strange beauty up here. It's found in deep-cut places. It's found in the smoke off the pyres and the pools on the abattoir floor.

Past their notoriety I knew nothing of the Slessors. When I went to the secondary school all I had to go by was common judgement and the air rucking up at the sound of their name. I was late for catching my bus home when I first came across Manda's group. The last bell had cleared the yard, except for a ring of girls by the playground wall, hair short and stiff, skirts high on their thighs. Their heels were scuffling and scraping on the tarmac. They'd got Donna Tweddle alone, tracked her down after a week's torturous promise of some retribution, for whatever reason she'd offended them: brains, looks, a boy. Manda was holding her by the throat and Donna drooped like rabbit-skin, like carrion. Manda's jaw was working up and down as she cussed. She knew her way round language I'd only heard outside the bookies or on building sites, things I'd only heard grown men say before. She was loud in what she was doing, but she was bonny in it too.

You're a lajful little tuss, she told the girl in her grip. Aren't you?

Her face wasn't pretty and smiling the way lads like girls' faces to be. Manda had her good features, those fire-dog eyes among them, and a heavy chest at fifteen, but that wasn't it. What she was doing suited her, and she was lit up, the way someone plain looks better when they sing, when suddenly it seems they have bright colours under a dull wing.

The girl was strung up against the pebbledash. I don't know if she'd tried to rail against the attack or to reason, but now she was holding still. Then Manda delivered a slap to her face. It was already aflame from her panic-blush, but the clean leather crack of that hand marked it scarlet. There was no real damage done. Manda waited until Donna began to cry, and at that point the viciousness went. She scratched a place under her chin, letting go of the girl's neck as she did so, as if she'd lost interest in finishing the lass off. As if she couldn't be bothered. The brightness left her too. Until that point she'd been full of glister. The girls in the group laughed and sang a last threat or two to Donna. Then their attention turned.

I'd stopped walking. I hadn't hurried away as I should have done, given such a situation. Manda Slessor faced me too. I was in her year at school but she didn't know me. I was a middle-row sitter, a nondescript. I thought she might shove me over or shoulder past. She did push others standing around her after she was done brawling, if they weren't on her side, if the temper was still in her. She saw me looking. I knew I shouldn't be, but I couldn't help it; I couldn't help thinking how bright she'd seemed. Her eyes curtsied quickly up and down, taking me in, a head-to-toe look in less than a second that said she didn't particularly like what she saw but it was no offence to her. I could feel the air all around, its softness, and in it the two of us were free to move. Her mascara was smudged in the corners from the day's wear. Her eyes were petrol blue, oily and volatile, ready to flare up and burn again. But they didn't ignite. She picked her canvas tote up off the ground and walked right past me.

*

I spent time up at the Slessors' house: High Setterah, it was called. I spent time with the family, after school and on weekends, whenever I could, because

I didn't want to stay out in the village I was from with my dad being moody and nobody else my age around. How it all came about I couldn't exactly say. The friendship was suddenly there one day, slightly askew in the beginning, like a sapling on the verge, then stronger and straighter. Maybe I was just someone she didn't get into a lock with, and that meant we weren't enemies. Or maybe she saw something she liked that day in the yard. She saw my admiration.

One day she caught me watching her eat a packet of crisps, licking salt off her fingers, and she blew me a kiss across the canteen as if she thought I fancied her. She could be daft and funny that way. Then we ended up sitting together in class. It was engineered under the impatience of our history teacher, who got fed up with Manda's constant giggling and barracking alongside goggle-eyed Stacey Clark on the back row. There was a space by me, with Rebecca Wilson being off poorly, and Manda got shifted.

Would you sit there and behave, please, Amanda, Ms Thompson instructed her, three times, each one louder and a little more desperate.

After tutting in the mardy fashion of a criminal playing victim, she screeched her chair out from under the desk and stalked over to my table. I got to see her up close for the first time, and her eyes were what my grandad would have called *ower glisky* – bright after the rain. She looked long at me. I knew it could go either way between us then. When you pen two animals in at short quarters they'll either take to each other and settle into company or they'll set to, gnashing and bucking.

Manda leaned over, clutching her pen tight and far down its stem, like a little kiddie would hold it, and she drew an inky scribble on the open page of my exercise book. So I put a scrawl back on hers. I did it without pausing – tit for tat. I saw she had a little heart carved into her wrist from a compass point, a thing which only the halest girls did. The scratch bloomed yellow-red, like a septic rose against her skin. Halfway through the lesson her biro ran out and she selected another from my pencil case without asking. She put it back when she was done.

Something was granted to us afterwards. We were past simply knowing the name of the other and what form we were in. We were allowed to say *Hiya* in passing, in front of our other friends, at the gates of the school, or in Castletown going down to the chippy or the arcade. Not that Manda needed permission for her friendships. She spoke to all manner of folk that were ordinarily off limits to the rest of us: the older, knotty-armed working lads who drove spoilered cars through town on their lunch breaks and knew her brothers to drink with; the owner and dealers of Toppers nightclub, and the tall, tanned girls who served at the bar there and trod that fine line between being queens and sluts with their reputations for giving good sex, bent over counters after closing time. Inside the old Covered Market, Manda spoke cheekily to the sheepskin-jacketed gents from Carlisle racecourse, as if they were her uncles, and they might have been her uncles.

And there was her mam's lot, the foreign cousins who came to the driving trials from Ireland, Scotland or Man, and brought with them piebald cobs, fiddles, rumours about filched electronics, litter and unfettled debts. The town banged on and on about their arrival each year, half of it discrimination, half superstition from a century before. How they were rain-makers and crop-ruiners. How they had curses or the Evil Eye. How they crossed the Border at night to the peal of the Bowness bells, said to ring out from their wath grave in the Solway when robbers were around, blah blah. Manda stepped into their loud circles and blagged cigarettes and gossiped and got invited to their hakes. She put up with nobody saying within earshot they were dirty potters and pikes.

No grand treaty was needed for her to know me. There came a day when I walked with her and a small crowd downtown for a gravy butty at dinnertime. I was standing near them in the cloakroom waiting for Rebecca to meet me, all of us putting on our coats and ratching in our purses for coins. Her face was dark inside the lum-pool of her hood, and she said, Come along on with us if you like, Kathleen.

What have you asked her for? one of the others rasped.

Because I'm fed up with your ugly mugs, Manda replied.

She and I walked together with linked arms from the Agricultural Hotel to the bottom of Little Dockray. Who isn't looking at us, I thought, and my heart was going at two-time.

The next month I was one room away while she got laid by a friend of the family – a jockey, who was married with kids. She reported back that he had a prick the size of Scafell and his come had run down her leg. Six weeks after that I sat with her in the clinic while she took two pills for her abortion, and I held her shoulders while she was sick. She said the nurse had told her not to look when she went to the toilet, but she had looked down into the bucket by her feet. It wasn't like period clots, just a ball of tubes. She said no bloody way was her mam ever to hear of it because her mam would've wanted the babby kept.

*

High Setterah was not the house of a rag-and-bone family. The grime of cart-claimed money had been swept back a generation by the Slessors branching out into carpets, property, equestrian prowess. Their travellers' heritage was easily remembered in a town which never forgot former status, but they'd grafted a fortune which made them untouchable by recession, competition, the bitter regional snobbery. The building was low and sprawling. It was almost a mansion except that it looked more like a Yankee ranch, with wooden interiors and a veranda. It had no business being built in Cumbria, one spit off the National Park boundary, and must have been forced past the council planners in the late seventies when the family was in its ascendancy, for it duffed all the local planning laws. There were paddocks front and back of the house for the horses, and slated stables off one wing of the property. Occasionally you could smell the beefy stench of Wildriggs abattoir wafting over from the industrial estate.

Inside there were too many bathrooms to count –

I was always scared I'd go in a wrong door – and pungent utility rooms where the Dobermann and the mastiff were kept. There was a sauna and a games room. Everywhere were hung ornately framed pictures of champion breeds, red ribbons indicating the annual royal downfall in the territory, brass reminders of the family sport. There was a long drive up to the house from the Kemplay roundabout and all alongside it were those glistening, hardy ponies, made stout by the gradient of fells, made tame at the Wall by the Romans, and now made fast by the leading reins of the Slessors.

Everybody thought it was Manda's dad who was the horse expert. And with his mule-neck and muscles straining as he bullied them across the beck at Appleby fair, they had no reason not to think it. Geordie was a master of saddlery. He wasn't well respected by the rest of the nation's breeders, the manor-house owners and Range Rover drivers, and that ritted him deeply. But they still came to him for advice and opinion on their steeds; they still bought his stock. He was always interviewed by the regional news stations after the trophies were won, his yellow Rolls-Royce parked prominently behind him. And though he had no right by birth or blood ever to own a car like that, he commanded the cameras in its direction, like it was the golden spoils of a chor shown off by a thief who knew cock to collar he would never get caught.

But it was Vivian Slessor I saw bringing stubborn geldings into the stables with brobs of fennel, in the old way of northern handlers. Her crop was seldom used when she rode. Though her racing and rutting knowledge was the lesser professionally, as a horse-handler she was somehow greater than Geordie – for her intimacy and charm, her hands working the tender spots behind the creatures' ears to quieten them. Geordie looked to her as his official bonesetter when a horse was damaged, rather than ringing the vet and being billed. He stood back as she bound up a foreleg with sorrel. One windy, mizzling day in April, Vivian Slessor first got me up into the saddle – on a gorgeous chestnut mare too big and blustered for someone of my size and inexperience. She softly talked and tutted as she led us round the paddock in the gale, and I wasn't sure if she was scolding the horse for cross-stepping or scolding me for bad posture. At the gap-stead of the field she unclipped the horse's rein.

Gan on, she said, and slapped its rump. Heels down, Kathleen.

She was the one who fed the dogs at night and

cured illness in the beings under her care. She was like that with her children too. She tended to them without complaint, with a kind of haughty devotion. The old man shouted at the hooligan lads to fucking grit down when they wrestled too near his showcase. He beat them for their cheek and backchat. But Vivian let them tussle and scrap for as long as it took them to thrash it out, until their raised blood got settled. She cleared up after them, wadded lint for the busted noses, collected the smashed plates strewn about the dining-room floor. From time to time she stood in court, in her tweed tack-suits and silk scarves, defending an accused son with that pure stare of hers. She had a gannan pride that told the judge he could never undo what she had instilled in her brood, that all the laws of the town, the curfews and fines, the borstal and jail time, mattered not.

But when she did light out towards her own in anger she damaged them badly. Not a one of them ever fought back the way the boys challenged Geordie for supremacy, on and off, if the chance came to them. She could turn loose a blue cruelty, and perhaps they all realised she was capable any day of murder. If she backed up her husband, an argument was immediately lost.

Get out and sarra them hosses, he might say to

Aaron or Rob, lazy with whisky, from his armchair in the corner.

The lad in question would chunter on about watching the footie, hating Geordie's cocksure orders. Then Vivian Slessor would brush a hand lightly down the back of her son's head and he'd rise up and put on his boots and go to the stables. It was a household of managed tension, and she was at its core. Vivian had a liking for modern things; kitchen appliances, music centres, cars; the sauna was built because she wanted scorching coals without having to go to a public gym. But she was a superstitious woman. Once I saw her take a set of metal tongs from the hearth and beat her eldest across his back for fumbling with her glass Luck. There was some old almanac to her world I didn't understand – belief in plant lore, ritual and sign, maybe some part of it Romany. Come All Hallows she hung dobby stones in the byres to keep the animals safe. She'd put up the roof of her convertible in clear blue skies if there'd been a kessen moon the night before. And she was careful where she'd allow the horse trailers to be parked in a town for the common ridings – never on a gallows hill, which was forbidden, though the horses were allowed to graze there.

I was fascinated to see the parents together. My

mother had died when I was eight and my dad never had another woman in his life, so it was an unusual thing, adult intimacy. There was something out of balance in the cottage where I lived, something steeply slanted. My dad had more heaviness to him than in just his arms and legs and the big belly where he rested his glass after dinner. But he was light compared to my mother's leftovers; her wardrobe of sour-smelling clothes, the elasticated jam-jars and dusty talcums. When I lay in bed at night and heard him grizzling I could feel the building pitch, trying to upend itself, and I'd brace my feet against the bottom of the bed.

The Slessors were even-weighted and indestructible. They'd paired by feral instinct, like wolves among us. If either of them stepped outside the marriage to a different bed – and there were those who gossiped about Geordie's liking for young stable hands, his chance bairns – then it did not threaten the union. They had produced between them three boys and a girl, all fit, all feisty. And there was a sense there might have been more, they had it in them still, he at almost seventy, she at almost fifty. The children bound them, but the two had bindings before, and bindings after. They belonged in the pairing. Even when you saw them singly in the house or around town you knew there must be another half, a mate. Neither went into it for money, for when they began courting there was none. Vivian had owned one dress that would serve for the wedding. All Geordie had possessed were a few tons of salvaged pipe and lead shingle.

For all his anger and brash, I never saw him raise a hand to his wife. He could have tried to brutalise her, the way he rode roughshod over everything else in life until it obeyed or broke. But he adored her, this rectifying woman. And he would, in any case, have met his match. He knew it. And, moreover, she knew it. If the man feared anything, it was his wife's genes, her cuntish atoms. I used to watch as she diced up chicken – the knife would slice and slice, clear of her fingertips, but she'd be watching him as he poured his Scotch. Though he'd likely never been near a history book in his life, it was as if Geordie Slessor knew the old region's legacy of women riding alongside men up to the Border, their babies twined across their backs in sacking. She would have taken those fists into her soft flesh, and even worn his black temper on her face in public for a while. Then in the night she would have slit him wide open, balls to bellybutton. She would've stemmed the blood with secret plant medicine, a draught to make the red come slower, and given him the guttings of his prize colt in exchange for his own liver. Or she'd have granted him something from her domestic realm of keeping the big house; a dinner of ground glass, meat frozen and thawed repeatedly, bannock of foxglove.

She was a handsome woman. Her brow was cross-hatched, but lively. Years before she'd had gorgeous tumbling locks, brown and gleaming in their wedding photographs. Perhaps it had thinned or greyed, for she now wore the unwilling bob of a woman proud for most of her life of her hair's beauty, and she'd still sweep it back, invisibly, off her shoulders. Manda got her full chest from her mam. Vivian was voluptuous, but bone-sculpted at her collar and her jaw. Men opened doors for her. And it was obvious when Geordie wanted her, for he made no game of it, he did not care who witnessed his desire. He'd come at her and grasp her waist. He might even have lifted up her skirts were she not to take it upon herself at these moments to move them both into a private space. Even then their sounds could be heard. After they were done they'd come back into the room easily, unashamed. Everyone knew when they were at it – High Setterah took on a different atmosphere. The smell of the horse sweat grew gamier. The boys became edgy and would take to drinking or baiting the dogs. Manda turned up the stereo.

But it was their tender moments that intrigued me most, the brisk expressions of what I took to be love, that would have been mistaken for ordinary occurrences or arguments by anyone not watching them as hard as I watched. Him pulling a spelk out of her hand, pinning her to the table with an elbow and twisting her arm behind her so she couldn't pull away while he doctored her. Him shouting at her from the car window for walking behind a reversing trailer.

Blind bloody bint! he spluttered. But it was panic in his voice, not anger.

And I saw her take out her husband's cock and hold it when he came home so drunk from the rugby club that he started to piss himself in the porch of High Setterah.

Of the two of them I preferred her, and this surprised me because women could make me uncomfortable and I didn't know what to talk to them about. But I would have eaten out of her hand without much fuss. Geordie, in a good mood, would flirt with me, and that I could take as acceptance of a kind, mortifying though it was.

Look at the lass, she's full up, is she not, he'd say, when Manda and I dressed to go out on a Friday night. Vivian often said nothing when I was in the room, but she'd sing songs with my name in.

Maybe I'll go down and see Kathleen,
A swallow comes and tells me of her dreams.
Soon I'm gonna see my sweet Kathleen.

*

Mostly when we went out it was around town, between the pubs, wherever Manda thought she might catch sight of a lad she was interested in. Sometimes, if one of her brothers didn't mind us coming with him on a delivery or to a gig, we went to the city of Carlisle. It was always a mad trip up, with stupid steering and breakneck overtaking, because the lads loved speed. They loved it on horseback, motorbikes, skis; any vehicle they could make accelerate to flatten their brains against their skulls.

There were two main roads from town – the old toll road, and the Roman, which was nearly disused and cut past the wither of Lazonby Fell. And there was the M6. It was a deserted piece of motorway – the last run before Scotland, so it felt like everything was petering out.

I'd sit rammed up against the window, my cheek pressed coldly against it, holding the seatbelt tight across my chest. Manda fought for control of the radio dials while one of her brothers drove. Usually it was Aaron, who would shoot the cambers as if he was on a private racetrack. We crossed that hinterland as people still do now, and they always have done, and they likely always will, regardless of police traps and cameras – moving flat out, at reckless speeds, as if being pursued.

I hated all the passages up to the city; that eerie twenty-five-minute slew. Something always seemed to be at our backs along there. These were the original badlands you were taught in school, if you didn't already know. You wouldn't want to linger. You wouldn't want to be caught alone, moving slow and obvious in the lowland. This was where the raiders met, coming south or north. This was burnt-farm, red-river, raping territory. A landscape of torn skirts and hacked throats, where roofs were oiled and fired, and haylofts were used to kipper children. And if you rolled down the window you could just about hear it – the alarms and crackling flames, women split open and screaming as their menfolk choked on sinew pushed down their gullets. The houses in the Borders, if they weren't fortified, were temporary, made of spit and cattle shit and wattle, easy to dismantle, because when the reivers came you either held fast behind eight hewn feet of rock, or you packed up and ran.

The van leaned hard round chicanes, forcing my cheekbone harder to the glass, with Aaron singing away to the Roses. Manda seemed fearless on the ride. She seemed to trust the run of things. But I imagined terrible events – wrecks and busted spleens. Adrenalin cleaved my brain wide open, and the giversum old county clambered in. It was said by trainers that up here the gentlest horse could nostril the smoulder of years gone by, taste clinker and burnt skin on the haunted vaults, and it might rear and toss its rider. And for all the Roman straightness, cars would often overturn. There were countless places where wreaths were laid. Even my dad, usually sedate behind the wheel, leaned hard on the accelerator with his mucky welly through these stretches, not checking the rear-view mirror. He'd fail to indicate when moving lanes; swerve hard as the Land Rover was swiped by gusts from the Pennines. Long-distance drivers, returning home to London and Birmingham, Stafford and Manchester, would often find franked letters from the Cumbrian Police, with points for their licence and a hefty fine, and they couldn't quite fathom why they were clocked going over ninety.

On several occasions Aaron Slessor almost killed us driving to Carlisle, and on every one I hated him a bit more. He kept the music loud and ignored us, except for the odd glance at my legs now and then. He went after hares on the tarmac, terrorised other motorists by sitting on their bumper until they moved out of his way. He'd take the back road along the moors, by the Caldew river, brackish as old copper, because it was straight and hummocked and he could try to get all four wheels of the van off the ground. He dropped me home late after each trip, where my dad would be asleep on the sofa with the telly turned low. Aaron didn't complain about ferrying me to and fro, he seemed just to like the drive, the fords and hairpins through the villages. Once or twice he'd ask for a kiss as I was getting out and I'd shove him back and say get lost.

You're pretty enough to lick out, he'd say. Stop being spooky.

At nineteen he was the youngest of the Slessor lads, and he'd an almighty chip on his shoulder about that, a desire to be the belted champion in the family. Geordie never got weak enough in his later years not to batter him. If anything he brayed him all the harder – the old family bull recognising his fighting days were close to over. That his youngest son took less interest in the horses than the others, while driving the Heltondales tighter on each racecourse's slalom, riled him no end.

Gudfernobbut twat, he called his son. Runty mutt. You'll amount to fuck all in this life, except laying rugs round fucking bogs.

Amateur brawlers from the town sought Aaron out, because it was said that to beat him in a fight was to take title over the town. He'd left school not a day after hitching sixteen, and started work at the carpet outlet. He was a looker, with the royal swagger of his old man. I'd seen him go to work on a lass. He had the ability to cut through what little pride she had, to strip her of common sense and condition her to waiting by the phone, waiting outside a pub in the rain, waiting for the characteristic bastard's alba a few weeks later when he'd got bored – telling her she had a dry quim, old biddy skin, fat belly, or spots on her arse, and that's why he no longer fancied her.

Nor was he discreet about his conquests. The details of them – the gasps, the games and sexual proclivities – were the chatter of the town for weeks after. How it had been in a horse-trailer and she'd knelt in fresh shit to suck him off. How he'd had her right after her sister in the same evening, a double-dipper. So that his circle of friends had the knowledge of any of his exes they needed before asking them out. And Aaron would occasionally revisit them, Friday nights, if something interested him enough in a bare leg or split skirt, a new look, a haircut. And they'd let him.

*

It wasn't common that I stayed home. They liked company, the Slessors. They liked having noise and new faces about them. I never felt unwelcome. But the summer after I got to know Manda my father started to notice me being gone. And he said it was a shame, him losing my mam and now me. The guilt made me hang around for most of the holidays, even though he was out rounding and clipping all day, the house was too chill for the season and it made me fidgety. In the mornings I'd phone up Manda, or she'd phone me.

Oh bugger, Kathleen, can't you come in? she'd say. I'm lonely. I'm going to get some new lippy. Fine, alright, ta-rah.

Then I'd go walking along a scrubby lonning in the village and up the Scar, knowing she'd soon be off into town, having a good time with someone else. From the summit I could see the beacon in the distance, trains dribbling down the main line, and the ponds of the trout fishery glimmering. On the way home I'd pass by a dilapidated farm, littered with rusting metal-seated tractors, derricks and machinery, tarpaulin strewn about in the yard. The owner of the place was a rare bastard. He could be heard in the evening yelling obscenities at his dogs and throwing their bowls at them. There'd be howls and yips and yelps. He had any number of hounds and collies, all rangy and greasy, and half-mad with the frustration you see in workers not put to the flocks.

The farm lay just past a dolt of brambles; I'd pass it after coming through the thorny lane, unsnagging my jeans with a twist of the hips every other step, my arms held overhead. It smelled of Swarfega and slurry, dirt and iron, and something sick, like industry and arable wrongly mixed. The man was known in our village for his bad treatment of animals, though he didn't keep many past the dogs, a handful of bantams, and the occasional pony or scabby penned-in pig. No one reported him to the RSPCA, for doubtless then they'd have to look into their own barns.

But one morning, near the holiday's end, I was walking past the farm's corrugated shed and I noticed the door was open. Usually it was shut and chained, with a thick trestle leaning against it. A dead horse was lying on the ground between the metal cattle chocks. The ground was slick yellow-brown, like concrete covered in piss and diarrhoea. I stepped closer, in under the gable, and a stink rose.

A shaft of sunlight lit the horse's body. The thing was a mess, shorn of its coat, with sores under its legs and keds crawling all over it. Its ribcage angled up through its flesh like the frame of a boat being dismantled. It had not stood for a long time for its hooves had twisted into thick discoloured spirals, like the nails of a Chinese emperor. For a moment I stood, stupidly looking at the creature. My brain began to flurry. It had not stood for a long time. It had lived on the floor; its hooves not wearing down from grazing and cantering like a properly upright creature. It had lived as it starved.

I took another step in and the horse snorted and moved. It lifted its head and rump together, tamping its torso down on the ground as if meaning to get up, and as it struggled its hooves clicked together and scraped on the floor like flints. It snorted out a pink foam that was lathered in its nostrils, and dragged its back legs again. Click-click. Then it was still.

I cast my eyes around for a pot of water, a blanket, some feed, and saw nothing of any use or comfort. I knew the farmer might be in the bothy, or bent in a shadow nearby, for the shed door would not have been open otherwise, but I couldn't see him. The horse lay unmoving again, as good as gone.

It's alright, girl, I whispered, to myself, or to the animal, I wasn't sure which.

Then I walked away. And then I ran.

With every stride, gall rose in me against the man. A dead horse I could have taken. I'd seen much worse – lambs stumbling on the howse, their eyes and arse-holes pecked out by the crows; hinds and heads stacked up inside the abattoir. A dead horse was not a problem. But I couldn't stomach a foully living one. My heart harried my blood as I ran. I pulled myself on through the blackthorn, tearing my arms off the burrs without untangling them. My mouth seemed filled with salt and seeds and pellets, though I tried again and again to spit them out along the path.

This farmer had driven one wife to alcohol, Vali-um and public breakdowns, and finally a bathtub overdose, it was said. The second had died after fall-ing into the silo. Neglect. Suicide, maybe. But a pa-tient killing in a reeking shed? No. A wife could up and walk away. She wasn't starved. Her feet weren't bound. This rotted, lying-down horse was worse than anything I'd known. It was something from a middle-forest fairytale, where the dark branches lift and in a clearing is Knife-Hand Nick, his children's heads bubbling in a pot above the fire. It was like meeting Nelly Wood in your dreams, when she stitches your skin to the hem of her cloak and flies away, dragging your pelt behind her, so in the morning you wake up flayed.

I stopped in the briar and leaned over and was sick.

By the time I got back to the village I was patch-worked with bramble gashes, and blood was dripping off my elbows. In my head I could still hear the skeltering hooves, scraping and clicking and scraping on the ground. I thought I'd go to the top field and tell my dad to fetch the vet. I thought I'd go into the house, take the shotgun from its rack above the mantel and kill the horse myself, or kill the man, or kill them both. But, like a reprieve, the blue Slessor van was parked outside the Fox and Pheasant, by the village green, and I saw Aaron climbing back inside from a delivery, or a pint, whatever reason he'd been there. He rolled the window down as I walked up.

Now then, Kathleen. What have you done to

yourself, you daft tuss? he asked, looking me over.

Nothing. Just come with me, will you? I said, and he laughed.

Aye, aye.

It's not a joke, Aaron. Come with me now.

He tucked his bottom lip under his teeth and had me stand there against the blue bore of his eyes. Then he opened the door and climbed down out of the van. Maybe he came for curiosity about the blood on my arms, already drying in black gobs from the summer heat. Or for the chance his sister's friend would let him move her knickers to one side, like he'd been after for weeks. Or maybe it was my tone, the bite of it, for I'd never spoken so assuredly to him before. Any other day I'd have been ignored, or he'd have flustered me with a tease. But he followed me through the ginnel, calling me a dippy bint, complaining he'd torn his shirt on the briar, and saying it better be worth it.

When we got to the corrugated shed the door was closed up and trestle-jammed again.

Give us a hand shifting this.

Dirty little spot you've got in mind, he said. You're a surprise, girlie.

I was shaking as we moved the timber, and breathing hard. He must have thought I'd become a lunatic, some lusty version of the girl he'd seen knocking about his house so many times. When I pulled the metal latch off its snick he put his hand on my back and gripped my vest into a ball of cloth, untucking it from my jeans. He stepped in close behind me and held my hips. I pulled open the door. The sun had moved over and it was dark inside, all spooled with shadow. The smell was throaty and rank, like something from a tannery, or a dog pound before the cages are hosed.

There, I said, as soft as I could. Can you see it?

Oh, in a minute you know I will.

He pulled me back harder against him, one arm belted across my stomach, one hand at the zip of my jeans. There was a pause. In my ear I heard a grating sound, like a piece of machinery slipping its driving gear. Aaron let go. He stepped round in front of me. Then he turned and drove me backwards out of the building, his palm splayed on my breastbone, pressing my nipple in painfully. I tripped on the concrete slab behind and went down.

Fuck off. Right now.

I looked up and he was standing above, pointing, his face in a twist, looking kiltered as if to hit me.

Fuck off home, Kathleen. It's not your business, this. It's not your concern.

Get. The fuck. Away, he said. Go on! Now! The muscle in his arm jumped.

I stood and stumbled off, thinking myself so horribly soft-minded, and only then did I feel my eyes begin to speckle and sting. I waited for him inside our cottage, with my cheek on the cold larder wall. I waited. But he didn't come. When I looked out of the upstairs window the carpet van had gone.

*

The next week I heard nothing at all from Manda. When I phoned the house Vivian said she was out and she said it in a tone that made me not inclined to ask anything else. Manda never phoned back. I stayed indoors. When I walked it was in the opposite direction to the farm.

The summer went on, and then it ended. By then I was sure they all must have taken against me for what had happened, for my babyish behaviour, and that was my worst fear. I thought about those times Manda had fought someone; the wet sound of knuckles against cartilage; the rows of double stitches required above her victim's eyebrows after she was done.

I took the first few days of the new term off sick,

though I had no fever and my dad suspected it. Then I worried this would make it worse. I imagined Sharon Kitchen and Stacey Clark huddled round Manda before registration like rooks on their desks, cawing in her ear that I was always a too-clever bitch, or they'd heard I'd called her a slag, and she should pull me down a peg or two. I knew all some girls needed as an excuse to start hating you was your absence, your lack of defence.

On my first day back she came to find me in the cloakroom. She stood next to me, the old group hovering by the door. I kept my eyes down. I heard her say my name. Then I felt her fingers digging in under my ribs to make me squirm.

No you don't, she said as I twitched away. Where've you been, you silly cow? Off shagging some mucky farmer?

When I looked at her she had a big smirk going. I knew she was pleased to see me.

Right. Come on, she said, putting her arm round my shoulders. Think we better have a quiet word – it's been pande-bloody-monium. Get lost, the rest of you. Ah, shit it, there's the bell! Meet you at twelve.

That lunchtime, in the bandstand in the park, Manda told me what had happened. Aaron had rung up their brothers from the Pheasant, and they'd come, because they always did come when it was put to them they had a duty. They'd searched the vicinity for the ratchety farmer – Lenny Miller was his name. She said the lads knew the fellow marginally anyway from the cockfights in the pits near Greystoke, and he was a sly git, so it was no trouble to them. They'd strung him up in the shed by his feet and cut the bastard with a riding crop right through to the putty in his spine. He was in Newcastle Infirmary, she said, not expected to walk again.

I searched her face for some sign of disturbance, and saw nothing favourable. Her eyes were that glisky blue, all bad charm and cheek.

I thought you already knew, she said. Thought you were just being canny and swinging wide. We've had the police up at the house about a million times. But it's just his word.

Manda took my arm as she always did. We walked through the park gates down into town, past the sandstone terraces and castle tower. She talked about the parties I'd missed that summer, the fairs and driving trials, and asked if I'd had any lads properly yet.

No, I said. I didn't get round to it.

Well, what you bloody waiting for? Or do you want Aaron to do the deed? Urgh.

As we walked I thought about the man, lying lame in a hospital bed.

What about the horse? I asked.

Manda shrugged. Her attention was on the building site across the road. A brickie in a red checked shirt whistled from the scaffolding. She blew him a kiss.

I knew if it'd been any other animal inside that barn, the Slessors would not have intervened. They wouldn't have done it for the kicked-about hounds. And they didn't do it for me. There was nothing sentimental to the family, nor could they be hired like mercenaries. It was simply the family's creed. It was luck, if such a thing could be so called. To slow-butcher a horse was an offence too great to let pass. Their spurs were buckled on and used accordingly.

Mam says you've to come for your tea next week, Manda said to me as we headed back up to school. The hornies will have gone by then and she'll take you riding. She's got a new pony for you. And you'll never guess what she's called it. Sweet Kathleen.

The Beautiful Indifference

Her lover had missed the train from London and would be arriving late. This was not uncommon after a night shift at the hospital. In the hotel room she studied herself in the mirror. The mirror was oval and full-length, in a hinged frame, which could be tilted up or down. She had bought a new dress. The blue was good on her, lighting her face and complementing her eyes. It was fitted through the bodice and waist but slipped to the floor easily when unzipped. He would like it. She finished making up her face, applying a layer of lip gloss, tidying the red spill at the corner of her mouth. Lipstick never lasted long when they were together; he would always kiss her just after she had applied it, as if he liked the smearing, viscous sensation. Sometimes she felt sure it was discomposing her that he enjoyed. She had lost a little weight since their last meeting. This was not deliberate. She'd been travelling a lot and had missed a few meals. The contours of her thighs and shoulders were pleasing. The previous night, after the reading, she had taken codeine and had slept well.

The room was hot but the window had jammed after opening only a few inches. Was this really designed to stop suicides, she wondered. Surely no one chose to jump from the second floor of a hotel. Better to use the bed, the bathtub. A soft pillowy ending or a wet red one. Outside, voices were loud in the street. The races had finished and people, made giddy by the early summer heat and grandstand cocktails, were shunting food containers into bins, shouting to each other about which venue to go to next. There was the sound of glass smashing, followed by juvenile laughter. Nearby a car alarm began howling. The tight northern gentility the city claimed for itself was coming unlaced.

She stepped away from the mirror and looked into the street. Light plumed over the buildings, a diffuse lilac glow like that which she had seen above the immense stonework of Paris on her first visit, coming up out of the Métro into its exquisite sordid heart. Perhaps they should go to Paris, soon. Or Florence. A last tourist carriage rattled on its way to the Minster, drawn by a white shire, the horse with its great, feathered hooves strutting on the cobbles. The driver leaned out from his position on the cab, talking into his mobile phone, shaking his head. A group of South Americans took photographs from the leather galley behind him.

The plan had been to meet and have a late lunch and then walk along the citadel walls. Now he would be coming here, to the hotel, and they would go out to dinner somewhere. It meant less time together, by a few hours. He would be catching the evening train back to London the following day. But perhaps it was better this way. Better to meet in the privacy of their room, so that they could be together for an hour, and empty themselves. A couple of times in the past the anticipation had led to problems; awkward exchanges, inappropriate behaviour. It had taken a few months to realise this initial discord did not mean incompatibility. She still found it remarkable: the spurs of desire, and the way desire interfered with all else. They were perfectly capable of having conversations, about politics, their occupations, anything. But they were not capable of corralling the animal necessity of ruining each other first.

She had recently mentioned this to a friend, not as a boast, more an observation, citing an encounter in a restaurant toilet, being discovered, and asked to leave.

Isn't it a bit ridiculous, the friend had replied, tending to her young child, spooning paste from its chin. You aren't a teenager. And actually, neither is he. Stop spitting out! What's wrong with you? You liked this yesterday!

Do you think it's unhealthy?

I didn't say that. Relationships are all defined differently, aren't they? If that's your thing. Anyway. Isn't it what you want, at the moment? Being with him means you can defer all the rest.

This had startled her. The tone. The implication that she was failing to make a sacrifice. Or that she had made a conscious choice.

What do you mean?

With exasperation the friend had turned away from the recalcitrant child, clattering the pot of orange paste and the plastic spoon down on the counter.

Oh, you know. Keep avoiding the hard stuff. Like this. The trouble is you probably don't have long left. Do you? And you act like it's not an issue. But everyone can see it is an issue.

She had noticed a change in the way her female friends responded to the relationship lately. At first they'd been enthusiastic, congratulatory, as if she were doing something avant-garde. She looked wonderful, they told her. She looked radiant. She should just enjoy it. But as the relationship had taken hold, becoming less casual, notes of disapproval had entered the discussion. Was it jealousy? Conservatism? She did not know. Perhaps she did seem ridiculous to them, now that it no longer constituted a fling, a desirability-affirming enterprise. Perhaps she was not entitled to the sex after all. Or the radiance. Men, on the other hand, had been unnerved from the beginning, as if she was not keeping to the natural order of things, as if she was performing an inversion. Or they had commented how lucky her lover was, recalling fondly an affair they themselves had had with an older woman during their youth. How they'd been taught a thing or two. After talking to them she was left with the dual feeling of being both transgressor and specialist. Only her father had been unreservedly for the relationship.

Darling, he had said to her, you should just let yourself feel something. If he makes you happy, be happy.

*

She stepped back from the window and looked at herself in the mirror again. The neckline of the dress was quite high. It gave the impression of thickening her collarbones. In the wardrobe hung another dress, belted and with an Edwardian-style bathing stripe, which he had seen before and liked very much. It was more fun, less chic. She reached behind and unfastened the one she was wearing. It drifted over her hips to the floor. She gathered it up and held it at waist height, paralysed for a moment by indecision, by aesthetics. Then she stepped back into it.

She sat on the bed. The book she was reading, or rather the book she had been carrying around for two weeks but not managing to read, was on the side table. She opened it and tried to get through a paragraph or two, but the words floated, the conceptual environment failed. She knew the author reasonably well; they had once shared the same publisher. Usually this motivated her to finish a novel – if only for the sake of etiquette. Often she discarded books. Whenever she made this confession people were astonished. It had come up again at her event last night. A woman on the front row had been appalled during the closing session.

How do we get our children to read more? All they do is play violent video games!

Why should they read? I don't. Given the choice I'd much rather do something else. Including blow things up.

You're joking? You can't really be serious?

Can't I? Why not?

Silence. Murmurs in the crowd. She was not adopting the correct role of advocate.

In truth, she disliked books. She felt a peculiar disquiet when opening the pages. She had felt it since childhood. She did not know why. Something in the act itself, the immersion, the seclusion, was disturbing. Reading was an affirmation of being alone, of being separate, trapped. Books were like oubliettes. Her preference was for company, the tactile world, atoms.

She shut the book. The cover was photographic, part of a female figure, a headless torso and limbs, though the novel itself was about the Second World War. The image was stock, meaningless. Give me a man, she thought. Give me the long cleft in his back. She had a popular science magazine in her bag too, which she had begun to buy in the last few months. But she had already finished the most appealing article about new-generation prosthetics. Soldiers coming home maimed were going to benefit hugely from new bioengineering techniques, according to the piece. The devices were becoming lighter, more flexible, intuitive of the brain's synaptic messages. It was as close to restoration as possible.

It was five thirty. The last she'd heard he had made it to King's Cross but he'd not texted since then to say which train he would be on. They arrived from London at twenty past the hour. The hotel was a ten-minute walk from the station; he had the address and the room number. Either he would be here soon, within a few minutes, or he would be another hour. She'd been primed the whole afternoon and now she felt fraught. She was unsure about the blue dress with its high neckline. She was unsure how it would affect the sex. Her mind felt white, empty of intellectual conversation. She could recall none of the finer points of the article in the magazine, though the subject, the idea of psychology and kinetics, had seemed fascinating. The noise outside was intensifying. Heels striking the pavement. Gales of singing. The thump of music from a pub.

She stood from the bed and looked at herself in the mirror. Her skin was luminous and secretive. She stared. After a minute or so her appearance became unstructured, a collection of shapes and colours. There had been no plan, not for any of this. Perhaps she had planned nothing in her life. And yet here she was, in this room, in this form. Speculatively, side by side in a crowd, she and her lover could be the same age. They had enough in common, and there was enough difference to make the relationship interesting. In practice there was no problem. But perhaps there was a flaw to the whole thing she hadn't seen, or was refusing to see, or which had not yet manifested. Children? Her friends now assumed what her position was.

She put her fingertips to her groin and felt along the ligaments and the gristle at the top of her thighs. The nodes were like unopened buds. She reached behind and unzipped the dress and it slid over her hips to the floor. She felt again, without the fabric barrier. Her body was full of unknowable cartilage, knuckled and furled material. Sometimes, when they lay together, his hands would unconsciously map her contours, pressing the organs and tissues. Or he would find her pulse in alternative places – the vees between her finger bones, the main arteries. He did not seem to realise he was doing this.

She was refastening the dress when the door lock clucked and released and he came into the room.

Hi.

Oh, hi.

He dropped his battered shoulder bag on the floor and came to her and kissed her.

Sorry I'm late.

Don't worry. I've had a good afternoon.

This is a nice hotel.

He greeted her again, softly, then stepped back. He removed his jacket and dropped it onto the bed. He did not look tired from the night shift. He never did.

His hair had been cut very short – there were lines along his scalp where the direction of growth altered. The last time she had seen him it had been long and curling around his ears, on the verge of being un-kempt, but very attractive. The smell of his wet hair was one of her strongest memories now. Like the feeling of deep humiliation for injuring the junior-school pet rabbit. Like the unhealing gash on her mother's cheek where hospital orderlies had caught her with a metal instrument while wheeling her to the morgue. Bracken burning on the moors.

Excuse me a moment.

He went into the bathroom and there was a trickle of water. In the time she had known him his polite-ness had never waned. Neither had her enjoyment of it. She glanced at her reflection. The eyes looked dark, shuttered by mascara. The smudged red mouth looked incapable of speech. Something inexact had hold of her. She tried to recall exactly how the nerves at the end of the amputated arm sent signals into the receptors of the bionic limb. How the brain was flu-ent in the language of electricity.

The shock of the real, she said.

The tap turned off and he came out of the bath-room drying his hands on a towel. He tossed the towel onto the bed, next to his jacket.

Sorry, I didn't hear you. What did you say?

I said, it's strange, each time I see you again. You look different. Altered. You're not like I remember. I have to get used to you.

He smiled. There had always been such invitation between them, always permission. He knew it. And her friends were disquieted.

You too.

Laughter through the open window. A police siren.

It's a little crazy out there.

The weather?

No. After the races.

How was your event? Did they buy books?

Yes. It was fine.

They were at each other's mouths a moment later. She was almost too small for the way he handled her. He liked the blue dress, he told her, it was beautiful, and the stitching, two or three inconsequential stitches, broke, as he lifted it over her head.

*

They went out and found a restaurant with courtyard dining and took a table. There was no chill in the air. They did not wear jackets, and the other diners, in their shoulder straps and short sleeves, seemed convinced that summer had arrived too. They ordered a bottle of wine. To begin with she was chatty and unlike her earlier indeterminate self. He laughed at her jokes. He asked what she was working on. She spoke briefly about the research and handed the subject to him. He had changed rotation within the last week and was now on the psychiatry ward. It wasn't yet very stimulating.

Aren't there some interesting cases? she asked.

There's a man who thinks he's involved in a conspiracy. It's all to do with a biscuit tin.

Is someone taking his biscuits?

He thinks people are communicating about him through the tin. Paranoid.

He lifted his fork and pressed his thumb against the tines, then looked at the three holes imprinted. He had a strong face. His shirts were never pristine. He seemed unmedical, too earthed. She could not imagine him at work, among the corridors and beds, the metal tables.

I'm going to become deskilled.

Deskilled?

Not performing procedures any more. You get rusty if you don't practise. Lots of ulcers to deal with, though. One woman won't get out of bed. She's too exhausted to speak. Her legs are a mess.

He continued to talk about the patients on the ward. The dementia, the bipolar and dissociative disorders. Those who showed no signs of distress about their symptoms. Freud's legacy. There was a woman who had been sectioned because her house was hazardous. She was hoarding all kinds of things: papers, cartons, tins, her own waste. The place was full to the ceiling and stinking. There were narrow routes through the piles, like a warren. There were rats.

I had an argument with another doctor about her. I'm not sure she should really be there. You can't penalise someone for the way they live. And she's not really a danger to herself, or anyone else. Unless her stuff collapses.

It does seem extreme. My father hoards. His attic is on the point of collapse. In fact it has collapsed. Do you think we all have a glitch? A condition, I mean?

Probably. To some degree.

He had ordered venison. It arrived on a white plate, a tidy maroon-centred shank in a shallow wash of pink. He usually ordered the most interesting meat on the menu – liver, foie gras, hare. She liked to watch him eat. He went very carefully through the dense tissue with his knife and worked across the plate until everything was gone. He would put the knife into his mouth if anything stuck to it. Three or four times during every meal he put the knife there, closing his lips over the blade, slipping it harmlessly along his tongue. The gesture reminded her of television footage of big cats picking up their cubs, lifting the slack bodies harmlessly between their teeth. She was not sure whether these erogenous qualities were noticeable to other people or whether they were simply her invention.

So. What's yours?

My what?

Your condition.

He smiled at her.

I want you all the time. Even right afterwards. I want to break you. It's a sickness.

She laughed.

Sadist.

Under the table, without having to lean too far, he found her leg. He let his hand rest there and with the other he continued to spear his food.

And what's yours?

She had been walking backwards in the pen without looking where she was going. She had crushed the rabbit's paw under her foot by accident. The thing had been pinned. It had twitched and tugged horribly under her shoe. When she'd dragged it from the back of the hutch to investigate the dam-

age its claw had been splayed and bloody. In a remarkable piece of social ostracisation, the whole
school had ignored her for a week, but she had not
been able to accept the punishment. She kept trying
to walk or sit with the other children, even as they
spoke among themselves about how stupid she was.

Pathological loneliness.

Really? Interesting. I've never heard of that before.

No. It clearly doesn't exist.

Because of what you do? The isolation?

She reached across the table and cut a piece off his
meat, from the end of the steak where the exterior
was charred and firm.

Oh. Probably because of where I'm from.

I'll have you certified and make a case study.

Great. Call it a syndrome. Give it your name. Do
you want to try some risotto?

Do you want me to finish it?

Yes.

You don't eat much.

I get full up quickly.

After paying the bill they left the restaurant and
walked a section of the walls. There was an applic-
ation on his phone that could photograph the night
sky and recognise constellations. They tried, but the
light pollution was too great, the stars indistinct.

They found a club and danced. The music was two decades old, difficult to move to though she knew the songs, and they gave up. They walked back to the hotel. The town had wound out. People were reeling through the streets. They passed a young man with blood running from a wound under his jaw. He was eating chips, impervious to the injury. A girl in a torn blouse was sitting on some church steps vomiting between her legs. Her hair was matted and dripping. A police car sped past almost silently, its rapid blue beam spiralling against the brickwork.

On the ward, she said. The ones who don't care about their illness – why is that?

Hard to say. It's either disease or conversion. It's not well defined.

He pushed her against the wall, slowly, kissed her.

In their room they stripped the heavy coverlet off the bed. The wine had numbed her. There was no pain. Her orgasm was small, towards the base of her spine. He moved her onto all fours. She watched him in the mirror opposite, his head falling forward, and to the side, his brow pleated, his mouth open. He was beautiful to watch. He withdrew and came across her buttocks. The semen was less thick; she felt it trickle as he lifted her up. His chest rose and fell against her back. He kissed her shoulders. He slept first and in the morning she woke and turned on her back and gently pressed against her pubic bone. She reached for more painkillers and the glass of water on the bed stand. She watched light gather in the room. So what if she had fallen behind? So what if she was out of sync? It might end. It might.

*

In the morning properly they went to the Minster. Another high blue day. The heat was already mature, suggestive of a later season. Men were jumping off a white Bayliner into the river. There were no remaining casualties and the town looked swept of debris. They walked past the riverside swans and geese, ice-cream vendors, picnickers, a funambulist practising between two trees, soft-shoed like a foal.

I read one of your books, he said.

Oh, right. When did that happen?

Recently.

Right. Which one?

There was a discussion. He had thought carefully about what to say. The analysis was astute. She could not tell if anything had altered in his perception of her because of the experience; she thought perhaps it had. Previously, she had doubted whether the work would be to his taste. Now she was not sure whether that mattered. Though he was not being critical, she began to defend the work, to play up its controversy. As if she had meant all along for the book to be problematic. The discussion became a political debate, which was easier. He took hold of her hand.

I'm having a fantastic time. I really like being with you.

She waited for a moment and then returned the compliment. They walked on.

People were sitting and lying on the grass around the Minster. Inside, most of the building was cordoned off, with a ticket booth controlling entry. They decided not to pay. They could see the colossal stained glass. Veils of coloured light hung over the nave. An official approached them.

First time inside, he asked. Well, it's good you've seen the windows now. They're about to take them down to start cleaning them. Lottery money. It's costing ten million pounds.

The official pointed out a few other noteworthy features inside the cathedral then courteously left them alone and greeted another group. They were both familiar with such places, had a secular interest. Still, the interior was impressive, the size and workmanship. Gold leaf and latticing. Stone tracts and arches, great masonic veins. It had been built without apathy, an estimation of God, Europe's greatest Gothic enterprise. She envied that certainty.

They lay for a time on the grass behind the cathedral, under the branches of a rustling beech, in reticulated sunlight. She lay with her head on his arm. They kissed, murmured to each other. They were lovers. She found herself counting the hours before his train back. After seeing him off she would drive north. Often the hours before parting were more difficult than the parting itself. He would quieten, and she would feel strangely enlivened, sheer, as if walking close to an edge. She watched the beech leaves flicker and interrupt the sky. She remembered then, something from the article about prostheses. That muscle had its own memory system. That consciously thinking about moving the attached arm, or the leg, would not move it. Those with new limbs needed to become unconcerned about articulation. They simply needed to let the body behave. She told him this. He had not read the article. He said that he would.

I had to help amputate a leg, during my surgical rotation.

Christ! I can't even imagine doing such a thing.

The vascular surgeon took care of most of it. I just

went through the bone. There were problems with the other leg. The patient died.

She lifted her head a fraction and turned to look at him. His eyes were open, staring straight up. She could see through the clear blue yolk of the nearest iris.

That's terrible.

It wasn't really the team's fault. These things happen.

He rolled his head towards her. In the sunlight they looked at each other brightly.

What you do, she said, it's amazing. I couldn't do it.

You'd surprise yourself.

No.

He gathered her in. The heat and smell and closeness of him was peculiarly surrounding, amniotic. Something opened in her belly, like a flower carved from air. She thought about the railway station, with its cyclonic roof, the moment when she would step back, the carriage door would beep and close, and the train would pulse as the engine engaged. Her throat began to constrict. She rose out of his embrace. She reached in her bag for a tablet and swallowed it dry.

I think my hangover's coming back. Might have to fight fire with fire. Drink?

Yeah, great. Let's go to one of the places on the river.

*

There was a small crowd outside the Minster when they rounded the corner. People were sitting on the steps, queuing outside the stall. At first it looked like a stunt, the horse hammering down the street, the empty carriage swerving behind, and the driver half standing, the reins gripped in his fists. The driver was calling to the horse, whoa, whoa, in a tone of irrefutable stewardship, but something was wrong. She took his arm and pointed. The white shire kicked on, coming towards the crowd, its hooves ringing heavily on the tarmac. It kept coming. The weight of the beast. Its breast working like a machine. Its fore and hind legs riving. Thirty feet from them the horse cut between two bollards and as the carriage hit tore out of its tack. There was the sick sound of brass and wood splintering. The driver flipped from his seat like an unbolted piece and landed lengths ahead. The shire kicked away, its reins trailing, its eye white-cupped and livid. It passed her at the exact moment she thought about stepping out with her arms held up. She felt its wake.

He had already broken from the crowd and was running towards the injured man. He was almost to him when she looked over. She hadn't seen him run before. For every human the action is never as imagined. Then he was kneeling, going to work. His back was to her. She couldn't see what he was doing. Checking the neck perhaps, or the head. The wrists, which had been held out like frail instruments to break the man's fall. His head turned slightly. He was talking as he ministered to the man, asking questions, or issuing instructions. Others began to arrive and cluster round, and her view of him was obscured.

She looked down the street after the horse but it had kept going and was gone. Spectators were walking purposefully towards the scene of the accident. They passed her, their faces set in expressions of shock and disbelief. Still she did not move. She looked after the horse. How real it had seemed, a truly designed thing. Someone would have to catch it before it damaged itself. She took a few steps, as if to follow, then turned and came slowly towards the glut of people. A woman was trying to steward, to move everyone back.

Give him some air. Come on.

Within minutes a medical vehicle arrived and two

jacketed paramedics made their way into the fray, one carrying a grey case. The bole of onlookers expanded and thinned. Information was passed between people. She heard talk of the horse having been hit by a taxi, or being spooked by a horn. She saw him. He was standing back, letting the paramedics work. The driver lay on his side, unmoving, then moving economically, but not his lower half. She did not approach. The paramedics stepped in and out, knelt and rose. He was walking towards her when someone in the crowd pointed over and a paramedic called him back. There was a consultation, or he was being thanked. He had been born the year she'd left home. That seemed impossible.

When they regained each other she embraced him. She did not know what else to do. The emotion was like fear, or the abating of fear, and it overtook her and made her grip the back of his shirt. She released him and he gave a brief report. The driver had probably broken a hip. There were bad abrasions. There was no trauma to the head. But he seemed not to care about his injuries. All he had kept asking was whether the horse was hurt.

*

She drove back across the Pennines. On the moorland the bracken was beginning to regenerate. Tight green spirals were coming up through the sea of dead stalks. The curled fronds looked ovarian. Like the illustration of these organs they had shown her to explain. Now the word and the picture and the bracken were the same somehow. She entered a belt of cloud. The light became more complicated, dense, unfiltered, west coast light. Her phone on the dashboard had chimed and was flashing. He always texted afterwards, to thank her. She would reply similarly. Then they would wait a few days before contacting each other again. She had begun to bleed, lightly. She could feel the intimate transit of fluid. The reassurance this sensation had once provided was fading. There was no meaning to it. She did not want to go back to the house yet and so she took a turning off the main road, south, towards her friend. She could call in without notice. The child meant they were rarely out, and it was not too late. She felt like telling her friend that it was wrong of her to have said the things she had. She was not deferring the hard things in life. Her friend was privileged and she did not know it. The assumptions were careless and because they were careless they were also cruel. She pictured a harsh exchange between them, bitter revelations, a dramatic exit.

But she knew she was not really angry with her friend. There was no point in trying to ground her frustration. No one was to blame. Retaliation would be unfair. She turned off the road again, this time onto a small country lane. She parked in a gravel lay-by and looked up at the hills. On the slopes the previous year's bracken was rust-coloured and collapsing, the fresh underlay was taking hold. With all the talk of carcinogens they did not burn it back as often as they used to. She had not smelled that fragrance in a long time. It would be dark soon. She knew she should visit her father, who did not live far away. But his endless hope would be too wearing. The cottage would be thick with dust and newspapers, unrinsed bottles. It would smell of mould and be full of loss. In her purse were the white boxes. After she had left the train station she had bought three packets of painkillers, from different pharmacies. It had been easy. Her mother had been the same age.

She had on heeled shoes from being in the city, from being with her lover, from moving among the public as if she was someone else. And the striped dress. What would they say about her attire, if they found her in the bracken? Perhaps they would say she had prepared. She sat in the car. She could still smell his wet hair, remember the feeling of its damp warmth between her fingers. Remembering their exchanges was like engaging in them again. The memories and the acts were almost the same. Whenever he came inside her it stung. Towards the end of their time together he would gauge how sore she was. He knew the difference between pleasure and discomfort, though the two were so closely aligned. She had brought him so close. And yet so much was unspeakable.

The hills were around her. She took up her purse, opened the car door and stepped into them. It was like opening a book.

Bees

One morning, not long after you've moved into the new house, you're out in the garden and you notice that the ground is littered with insects. They lie here and there, like dark smuts between the tawny southern pebbles, leggy and fine-winged. There are dozens and dozens of dead bees. You were attending to something on the ground, a weed perhaps or a blown sweet wrapper, bending over to pick it up, and now, scanning the earth, you can see the creatures strewn all about. Stiff, fossil-looking things. Black-capped, like aristocrats at a funeral, their antennae folded, with mortuary formality, across their eyes. Around their bodies are bands of gold. Some of the bees have their back sections missing. Some are lying in two equal pieces. Some are perfectly whole, as if having landed from flight in a timely fashion, just at the end of their lifespan. You kneel. You examine the creatures. Up above you, the hedgerow towers. The people in the house next door can't see in. This tiny London garden is a secret cemetery. You are the only mourner.

*

It is fair to say that since arriving in the city you've been noticing details. You've been gathering them up, storing them away. You're a receptacle for information. This is a new disposition for you – this vacancy. Always before you felt full, heavy with what had made you and who you were. You wonder if it's a prerequisite for living in the metropolis, the scraping out of past existence to make way for a new, enormously complicated one. You are a recent settler. You've come down from the far north. You've left behind the yellow moors and drenched fields. You've left the people who know you, who have reared you, inured you.

It's not work-related, this move; not a new job, that which beckons most rural emigrants. You've come away from your old home for another reason, a reason you imagine to be prosaic, here in this cauldron of life. You've come to forget, to move on. And with this move, some lurid internal part of you has unzipped your flesh and stepped outside. A red, essential thing. You felt it go. It happened as you were getting off the train in Euston station, standing on the platform and reaching back into the carriage to collect your suitcase. There was a sudden internal event, like cramp or a stroke, like waters breaking. Something rose up inside your chest. It split you open. It tugged itself through the walls of muscle, slid to the floor and moved off into the crowd. What's left now is a loose pink sack of human being, bearing your name and your forgettable history. A skin bag with a few organs and some blood slung in; viscera, which cooperate only to the extent they must, in order to keep you alive. In truth, it's a relief. This downgrading of self. This degeneration. You don't ache or feel hunger or long for anything. You don't mind going without that prime red aspect. You have been granted mercy.

*

You shuffle around on your knees in the garden, place your hands down and lean forwards. There they are – the bees. They are strangely composed. They seem to have collected in groups, selected communal places in which to expire. You pick one up by a crooked leg and place it in the palm of your hand. A dry bristle. Teasel. Half-burnt paper. What is it that has killed them? Is it something to do with infected hives? Mites in their throats or pesticide? Is this the beginning of the holocaust that will lead to the death of grass and cattle, the collapse of the pollinated food chain?

You're lucky to have the garden, of course. You're lucky to be where you are now. It could all have been very different. A bedsit in Hackney: depositless and rank. A doorbell rung, suitcase in hand, the rationale that your one retaliatory indiscretion months ago may have resulted in meaningful fondness of some kind. The man in the doorway looking at you, trying to remember, and his girlfriend calling from the kitchen, *Honey, who's there?* You've landed softly in the hardest of all cities, with only a few possessions, just what you could carry, and a freshly gutted body. Your oldest school friend took you in, her flatmate moving out just when you needed a room. You paid two months' rent up front, though she said you could owe her. You didn't flinch over the price.

She's another northerner, this friend, from the same soaked valley but one village over. You've kept in touch with her since school, to some degree or another, depending on each of your situations year in, year out. In school you were good friends. You would go out in the local town at weekends. She was pretty but never as lucky with boys. Once the two of you got drunk and kissed but it was a moment so unreal you've never talked about it; you might even have invented it. She did well in school. She's a professional now and her dialect's been rounded off, softened at the edges. She works in the publishing industry, marshals authors from one event to another, puts up with egos and tantrums.

You visited her a few times prior to moving, though it was hard getting away from the farm – you had to use Christmas shopping as an excuse – and you blew off steam down here. You always liked visiting the city. You liked the throngs of people, the anonymity, the lattices of wires and trains, the energy. While down here you complained about the pettiness and insulation of the Borders, said you wished you'd left when you'd had the chance. *You can still come down,* she told you. *People do it all the time.* You shared fond memories of school and fell walking, old men's pubs in the villages, lost boyfriends, the ones you lost your virginities to. You filled her in on local gossip, what such-and-such was doing, who such-and-such was screwing. You cried, and, wordlessly, she comforted you. She came to your wedding, ten years ago. She saw the whole thing, the overturned table and the broken glass. She knows about the circumstances of your moving here, but only as much as you've conveyed. She'll not ask more. She'll wait for you to broach the subject. She's from the north.

After the great heathered fells, the watery expanses and the lowlands of your home county, this garden seems tiny, condensed. There's a bench, on which you are now sitting with a dead bee in your hand. The bench is being molested by untrimmed bushes, buddleia, you think, though you're not good at recognising such plants. A Mexican pot-bellied stove sits up at the top end by the kitchen window. There's a bird table. Plant pots. These things belong to your friend, who has been in the city for almost twelve years, long enough to make it her home, long enough to acquire possessions and a good social circle. She has secateurs, a trowel, packets of broom and violet seed. She tends the garden to relax after work. But her hours are long, she often has to go out in the evening, to festivals and launches; she is away much of the time. You have the place to yourself, which is good, in a way. You've been out into this cultivated pocket of nature quite a few times. Mornings, to catch the hazy sun as it breaks free of the rooftops. You're not yet working, though soon you will have to find a job. You've had glasses of wine out here at the weekend, with your housemate: she's keen to give you company when she can. It's then she tries to tell you it'll be all right, her propositions brief and un-assailable. You always nod. *Yes, it's for the best. Yes, there'll be others. Yes, you are in your prime.* You've been out here at night when you can't sleep – the bed still feels strange, sleeping alone still feels strange – or to cool down, London's summer being more humid than you'd expected. And you've also come out to investigate the nocturnal barking and rumma-ging, the eerie yowling, noises that seem out of place in this urban setting but to which you are attuned. The moon in the city is vast and unwhite.

These are the moments when you wonder whether coming to London was the right thing – these disturbed, sleepless moments. The north seems close, connected as it is by darkness and light, by bit-ter constellations. It's been difficult to reconcile the permanence of this change. It's been difficult to let go, to forget entirely. At night, in the garden, it oc-curs to you that it might have been your heart that left you as you reached the capital. Your heart might not have travelled well, closed up in its cavity, quiv-ering and gnawing at the bars of your ribcage during the commute. It might be tracking north now, along edgelands, past spoil-heaps and stands of pylons, under motorway passes, back to the higher ground. Back to him.

During the day you go into the city because it's a place you're supposed to go into, now that you're a resident. You encourage yourself to learn bus routes, find groceries, independent cafes. You go to galleries and shopping districts. You share the pavement, walk with or against the crowd. Sirens. Traffic. Planes. There is such different choreography from that which you are used to, the slow machinery in the black fields, livestock cropping the tufts, your once vernacular scenery. You've some money and a credit card that has not been stopped. Soon you'll find employment, probably quite menial; you're not highly qualified, but for now you're acquainting yourself with London, distancing yourself from the time before. It is a faceted city: ornate, sooty, modern. You aren't afraid of it. You note things, place details on a cerebral shelf. You memorise noises, chimes, electrical thrums, the euphonic character of the place. And smells: the stale pavement, body odours, doorstep musk, green ponds. There are underground winds, motion sensations, beeps, commands. Your head has begun to fill with urban miscellanea, civic clutter, like keen junk.

*

But this waste of bees is unexpected. You're interested in the particularity, the mystery. You stand up from the bench and drop the little carcass from your hand. You walk about the garden, your eyes cast down, wondering what kind of disease might have decimated their community. There were those terrible rains shortly after you first came, that swelled the Thames and the Victorian sewers past capacity, that bloated fish and sent them up, silver-bellied, to the surface of the brown surge. You don't understand the natural calibration here, not in the way that you know fell ponies graze the uplands in summer and riverside in winter, sheep will remain hefted until struck off, and the swallows come back in April, feeding on the wing above bright streams. In the garden you tread around the bodies carefully, agriculturally. Then you go back inside the house.

*

The days pass; warm, sticky summer days. There are thunderstorms. The sky above London turns purple, then grey. Rain sluices from gutters and culverts, spills from eaves. The storms pass, the dark patches in the roads shrink. You go out on a few dates. These men are used to dating. You are not exotic. One night you go home with a man and you fuck him. Or, you let him fuck you. He does it hard so as not to lose his erection. Halfway through he withdraws and asks if he can take off the condom. You say no. Then you say yes. Two days later you come down with a bladder infection. You go to a clinic for antibiotics. It takes hours, by which time you are urinating blood. For a week or so you think about going back to the north. The regret passes. You sit outside in your shorts and a vest. The sun is strong, liquefying. You relax. The garden remains littered with bees. You never see them dying. You don't see them tumbling from the sky, or twitching on the ground, pedalling upside down on their backs, their frail wings vibrating into stillness. They are simply corpses. All you witness is evidence of their extinction.

You go into the garden more frequently. You watch the ones that are alive, moving like Zeppelins in the air, scooping inside the flower heads. There are plenty. They seem oblivious to the bodies underneath. It is business as usual. When you are inside the house you pause at the bedroom window and look out, in case a clue might present itself. You go down to the library by the park to gather information about apiculture. You read about dangerous breeding techniques in America – the weakening of certain species. The almond industry, bees flown in on jumbo jets to pollinate. You read about particular kinds of beetles that burrow in under the eggs and attack juveniles. Bees are highly cooperative. Any sickness, any threat to the queen, is dealt with immediately. They will sacrifice themselves, clean out infected combs with their mouths, fly as far away as they can before dying. But you've looked over the garden hedges and fences along your street, even in the allotments nearby, and there are no hives.

*

You arrange interviews. You move your voting registry, put your name on a waiting list for a GP. You know you live in London now. You still feel empty. And you still wonder about that red thermal mass. All the anger and desperation and love that was furled up inside you, making you wild for the last few years. Where is it? Sometimes you think it can't have gone far; must be roaming London, scorching and singeing the undergrowth as it moves. Or is it in your old home, back in the house that you shared, with its slippery courtyard and hay-smelling outbuildings? It could be curled up in front of the coal stove next to his dog, or staring out of the front door at the Scar as the authentic rain comes down, or bumping about in the passenger seat of the Land Rover, driving into town. You wonder about him, what he's doing. If he's managing. If he's thriving. If he's sorry. If he knows that he might still own your busted-out incendiary heart, and that you're turning through this new life as uselessly as a shed tractor tyre.

As you get ready for your first interview you look at your face in the bathroom mirror. It's lined along the brow, around the eyes, at the corners of your mouth. It's the face of a person who has spent time outdoors, in all weathers. But you have always made an effort with make-up and you are attractive. Once you were considered very attractive. You were his prize. You aren't old for this city, where youth stretches out into middle age, where people don't commit or own mortgages or cars. You felt older in the countryside, comparatively. Old in your hometown, where women the same age had children already sitting exams or getting pregnant themselves. You have no children. You might have had children. You were at risk of having them young. But you didn't want to, even though he did. He said it was the right thing to do. He imagined extra hands to help around the byres, a son to come to the pub with on Christmas Eve.

But something in you stalled. You resisted. You kept taking the pill, every day, 6 a.m. And you had one abortion, secretly. You took the tablets and wore an incontinence pad and slapped the paleness out of your face and went to the pens to help with the clipping. It wasn't even about him, the decision, though you could have set it against his temper or his drinking, his heavy-lashed eyes that were cast over the rumps of other women, and his dirty nails that must have dug into them too. You just didn't feel broody, didn't feel the inclination, that ache in the space between your arms. You never saw through a full conversation about it either, you always made an excuse. The dogs needed feeding. You had an appointment in town. *Talk about it later*.

But you never said no when he wanted to. You maintained an active sex life, from the last year of school until that sore red ember began to glow. He liked you to unfasten his blue boiler suit and pull it down off him. He liked you on your knees, on the floor, liked to put his hands against the wardrobe and look in the mirror, at your head moving, at his length and the hard muscle in his stomach. You can remember the taste of him now, from years of practice – sour, salty. *Yeah come on, swallow me. You're a good bitch*. You can remember the smell of silage and diesel in the farmyard, the feel of him butting behind you, increasingly minimal in his inquiry, complaining if you weren't wet enough, pulling out and moving it into a tighter place. A bonny pair: that's what they called you. Best match of the town. You knew what it meant, to be with him, to be his. You signed the contract.

And he breached it. A slap or two to begin with. Public argument, things that couldn't be unsaid. An infection passed on, him saying it was you not washing properly. Then the rumour, the pregnancy, the local slut. It lit you inside and smouldered your innards hotter and hotter, until the bloom got livid. But you bore it, kept it in, even seeing that other woman round town, yes pregnant, being called frigid outside the Rafa club when you tried to take him home, the tenderness at the back of your throat from choking on him, being forced to. You bore it, until you couldn't bear it any more. The one-year-old daughter – paid for informally, you found out – black-lashed and beautiful just like her father when you finally saw her. You initiated a confrontation with him. And got one. And the police too. One of whom was his cousin, who filed a dodgy report. The courts were not involved. Hard times for farmers. Work stresses. Mitigating circumstances. You packed a bag, got the money out, and left. He's not come down to find you, with his shitty wellies or apologies or demands. All that remains between you both is that historical red piece that clawed away and is missing somewhere now, that urgeful hybrid creation, carrying flames along its back as it moves. You look at your face in the mirror. Still attractive. You wonder if you'll ever be able to use your body again for more than basic living.

*

You don't get the job. There are one hundred and sixty other candidates. They tell you as soon as you've interviewed that you are under-qualified. They suggest taking some unpaid internships, though the competition for these is also fierce. You go home. Your friend is away overnight at a festival. You open one of her bottles of wine and sit in the garden and drink it. You sit on the bench and look at the dead bees. You collect a few and put them on the seat beside you, arrange and rearrange them. You sit for a long time. The moon is dilated. It is enormous. A supermoon. It is as close to the earth in its orbital ellipse as it's been for ten years. You know that the Solway tide will be affected. The haaf-netters will not go out and tread the sands. There will be curious minor occurrences. A dead hawk, perched upright on a fence. Lame cattle. You finish the wine. You watch the moon set. You lie down on the bench and sleep.

In the morning the sun is warm. Your head hurts. Your neck is stiff from lying on the wooden slats and your arm is completely numb. You have slept for only a few hours. Carefully, you sit upright. Then you see it. There, in the corner of the hedge, is a disruption of colour, perhaps ten feet away from where you have been sleeping. You think at first you must be mistaken. But you are not. It's a fox. It is a rust-red, blaze-red fox. And it's big, though it seems juvenile, with oversized ears and paws. It's sitting upright, arch-jawed, snouty, and is scanning the garden with brilliant topaz eyes. You hold still. You try not to make any sounds. It is not looking at you, though it must sense you are close, must have assessed the degree to which you are or are not a threat. You are tolerable. It's looking at something else. Your housemate told you there were foxes in London, lots of them, brash urban scavengers responsible for tearing open bin bags, pungently scenting their patrols, so tame you could almost play with them, but you didn't really believe they were so fearless.

You've only ever seen foxes in the north before. There they were pale orange and discreet, sloping along roadsides, diminutive on the moors, or cowering from the hounds. This one is unapologetic, going nowhere, as if it owns this city enclosure. It is as if the creature has been stoked up from the surroundings; its fur like a furnace, eyes sparking. You watch it scan the air. It follows the heavy, resinous flight of a bee. It is a candid little hunter. It crouches for a moment, then springs up on its back legs. The jaws open and snap shut, and as it lands it shakes its red head furiously.

The Agency

The children had left for school an hour before. I'd cleared up after them, putting stray, dusty socks into the laundry basket, rinsing plastic yogurt pots and stacking them in the recycling bin. I'd had time to shower, dress, make myself some coffee, and was about to turn on the computer. On the display screen of my phone the number came up as Private. A polite male voice asked if he was speaking to Hannah, and if I knew where to come. I stuttered and hesitated. There was a long pause, unbearably long it seemed, filled only by the insectile pulse and tick of the satellite connection. I thought about hanging up, and switching off my phone, but finally I said, Yes, I have the address. Thank you. Thank you for checking.

Of course, he replied, his tone even, as if he was used to transactions of gratitude.

I remember thinking afterwards that the call had been well timed. It was considerate. In some small way this was reassuring, though I was still uncertain about following through. It was one thing to have found the nerve to call the number on the back of the card that

Anthea King had handed me. It was another altogether to dress myself smartly, as I knew I would, get into the car, and drive fifty miles into the city. For the sake of what? A change in my life to which I was not entitled, and was not even sure I wanted to make. I had no idea how long the appointment would last or what it would involve. And if it had not been Anthea who had made the recommendation, I probably would have put aside the idea.

But she had assured me that there was no chance of anything unprofessional occurring. The company was private and reliable, and she had been a member for over a year.

It's a nice term, isn't it, *member*? she had said during one coffee morning together. The Agency is like that. Everything feels very tight. Very secure. Life rarely offers us these opportunities without making a hell of a mess afterwards.

I'd looked across the table at her. Perhaps I was looking for excitement flinting at the back of her eyes, or desperation, because I felt myself to be increasingly desperate. Her hand was cupped around the china mug, her thumb stroking the dark smudge of lipstick on its rim. She was smiling. She appeared unruffled. She could have been talking about anything – a yoga club, a salon.

Don't look so tense, Hannah darling, she had said. Really. You deserve this. Everyone deserves contentment. You have to look after your health. It's amazing how truly discordant life seems if you feel wrong within yourself. If you feel lacking.

Her smile lengthened, and I thought, as I always did in her company, that she was a very attractive woman. Her hair was tawny and full, expensively fletched with auburn, and it sat brightly against her blazer. From behind she might have been mistaken for a young woman, trim and energetic as she was. But her face was heavily lined. If anything she looked older than her actual years, perhaps by almost a decade. Her attitude remained youthful, animating the mature, textured face, and it was this combined quality that was most appealing. Men flocked around her at parties, topping up her glass and listening to her upbraid politicians and culture ministers, as she did in her weekly newspaper column. Her laughter rang above the noise of any gathering, rich and inelegant.

I'd known Anthea since the children began primary school. The other mothers had probably assumed she was grandmother to the little girl, Laura, whose hand she was holding. And until the child said, Kisses Mummy, and pulled her down so she could reach her cheek, so had I.

Well, now we can all return to our bloody lives, she'd declared slowly, once the sons and daughters were beyond the school gate. She'd caught my smile and snorted, putting her hands to her mouth. A week later we had exchanged telephone numbers. Soon after we began socialising as couples – our husbands knew each other by sight, it turned out, from the university campus. She introduced me to a new group of women in the town, a vibrant artistic set of varying ages, who went into the city intermittently, to work, to attend book launches and ebullient, champagne-driven gatherings. A couple of them were journalists, one was married to a radio presenter, and one worked in television. They were all friendly and, if not uncommonly beautiful, were svelte, fine-boned, and bought rich, top-end cosmetics.

I liked them, and they in turn seemed to take me under their collective wing. Often we would meet on Saturday mornings, at one of the small pricey boutiques in the centre of town. Expensive shirts and gowns would be fitted, and occasionally bought. The women complimented each other, were honest about what was flattering and what was not. They were casual around each other when undressed.

Chesca, look at your perfect breasts. Can't quite believe you've had three children!

Darling, go a size down, that's hanging off you like a widow's frock!

The lunches afterwards were always wine-accompanied and there were confidential exchanges; often I would return home sparkle-eyed and flushed, and John would make coffee and tease me about my alcoholic friends. There were annual parties hosted at Christmas, New Year, and Midsummer, or held for charming aesthetic reasons, like the flowering each May of Tamar's red peonies; occasions strictly observed by the group, and around which other family holidays were planned.

At the first of the Saturday lunches I had been slightly shocked by the level of confession. John and I had become a self-contained unit; any upsets or difficulties were locked away, resolved internally, or not. As they skilfully deboned fish and forked their way through salads the women swapped not only old pieces of jewellery but medical histories and marital frustrations. Health scares. Stories of previously loved men. The desire for more rigorous forms of sex. Tamar spoke of an affair she'd tolerated, and her husband's eventual recommitment.

The thing is, he was stupidly transparent, she said, laughing and shaking her head. Edward thought I wouldn't know exactly what it meant when he was sitting there in his chair moping. She hadn't rung him for a week. I ended up comforting him for whatever ridiculous reason he made up, missing the dead dog or something, but I knew full well why I was really comforting him!

Noticing my expression, she had smiled at me, waving away my sympathy and my concern.

Oh, don't worry, Hannah. Your John worships you. He isn't the type. And he certainly isn't an idiot.

I wasn't sure that she knew John, but her kindness and flattery touched me. Then her smile tightened a fraction.

Women can live far more comfortably with secrets, don't you think?

It was Anthea who replied. Yes. And may we remain unreadable.

She held up her wine glass and the others toasted the sentiment.

Afterwards, as we tottered towards the taxi rank, Anthea told me that each of the women idealised another in the group, for their looks, their vivacity, or their maternal skill. I wondered whom she most admired – perhaps Lizzie, who was fifteen years younger, was a successful playwright, and had had a series of overlapping, adventurous relationships that Anthea delighted in, calling them 'jolly friendships'.

Then I wondered if she was referring to me, and the way I would often study her during our coffee mornings. There was a fascinating Englishness about her, redolent of previous generations, of grandmothers who had been in their day industrious and spirited. Her fund of cheer was immense and remarkable, even in the face of her own divorce, which she strode through dauntlessly, it seemed to me, six months after I had met her.

Bloody men and their bloody egos, was her summary of the situation. They'd rather make love to themselves than their wives. Is it any wonder we're driven to acts of madness?

But there was something more to her than this gently decadent style. Early on I'd noticed an odd, recessive tilt to her personality, a watchfulness. When she was not joking or flamboyantly uncorking a bottle, she was extremely good at being dormant. She could sit at the end of the table, in almost predatory stillness, for an hour or more, while conversation went on around her. Everything seemed poised in her then, her handsome, mobile face set, and only her eyes moved as she surveyed the scene, marking, biding. She was usually the first to receive a phone call from anyone in the group having a crisis, perhaps because of her age and experience, but mostly because she never issued judgement, merely good advice. And she was discreet. Gossip about the others never really came my way through her; though once aired she was happy to speculate. I'd always felt I could talk to her about the most difficult, painful things.

*

She had not given me the business card immediately. It was not issued with the air of prescription, as soon as I'd confided in her, about the discontent, the affair with John's brother I had almost entered into. The morning she handed it to me we had been discussing something else entirely, something irrelevant – the latest atrocities in the war, or sugar in our children's cereal. At a natural pause in the conversation she reached into her purse and took out a neat white rectangle.

This is for you, darling, she said, passing the card to me. One shouldn't have to go on feeling so embarrassed about oneself. I am a great believer in private acts.

Printed in black ink, the listing simply read *The Agency*. There was a number below with a mobile phone coding.

Do ring, she said. This is for reception. Ask for an initial consultation. They can set something marvellous up for you, and then you'll have a direct line.

I must have appeared conflicted, because she reached out and laid her hand over mine. Her fingers were soft, but the grip was firm. She still wore her diamond engagement ring.

Darling. You must. It isn't what you might think. Not at all. These things consume us until we do something about them. Trust me.

*

The first appointment was scheduled for eleven o'clock in the morning. I had arranged for another friend to collect Jamie from school, and keep him an extra hour, in case I was delayed. Katie had a swimming class and would be late home anyway. I wanted to give myself time to recover, if that was necessary. I could have asked Anthea to look after them, but for some reason I was hesitant to tell her where I was going, as if it would have furthered our conspiracy somehow, made her culpable.

I'd been planning what to wear all week. I'd settled on a burgundy suit that I almost never put on any more, bought from a boutique in London after I'd received a surprisingly high severance package from my last job. It still fitted, though the waist was snug. Several times I'd taken it out of the wardrobe and hung it on the back of the door to admire it, only to rehouse it under the plastic dry-cleaner's sleeve. There was a black silk brooch pinned to the lapel of the jacket from a Remembrance supper that John and I had attended at his college the previous year. I'd bought some new black shoes, with a heel slightly higher than I usually wore. I'd also bought new stockings, which I left in their packet inside the shoe-box at the back of the wardrobe. It all felt slightly ludicrous, this fancy preparation. Half of me recognised it as such and was internally withering. I felt unqualified. I was not like Anthea King, did not possess her tailoring, her vigour and courage in life. I had always been a stiff dresser, never quite able to wear my best clothes with the sort of confidence she and the others had. But part of me was thrilled to think of the suit draped from its hanger, the silk sheaths folded carefully around their cardboard tongues, and the unscratched shoes facing each other in the box, their heels spearing the tissue paper. It was exciting to imagine I could step into the outfit.

The morning of the appointment passed quickly.

The children left for school, their books and lunch-boxes slung into their bags. I watched John wheeling his bike alongside the house, his rucksack on his back, his hair parted by the fresh breeze to reveal a seam of white scalp.

Blowy old day, he called to me through the kitchen window, the gravel path crunching under his feet. I waved, and he was gone.

I had been awake for much of the night, lying on my back, staring at the orange glow from the street-lamp. Once I had reached out to touch my husband's leg, the crisp hair on his belly. I'd moved my hand down nervously, but he was sound asleep. I'd drifted off around five and the alarm had woken me with a start an hour later. The satisfying care with which I thought I would prepare and pin up my hair was absent. I dressed hurriedly and was ready earlier than planned, then felt unfocused, unable to concentrate on anything. I took two paracetamol and made more coffee. Then I cleaned my teeth again and reapplied lipstick. When I looked in the bathroom mirror my appearance seemed hawkish. I realised I had forgotten to apply concealer around my eyes. I took the silver tube out of my make-up bag, dotted it on and blended the cream.

It was not until I was in the car, on the bypass

heading out of town, that I started to consider the price of the excursion. Money had not occurred to me at all. I hadn't inquired how much the procedure would be and no initial fee had been given on the phone. Anthea had not mentioned money either, but of course she had fewer financial concerns. The divorce must have benefited her, or perhaps she had inherited; she owned the town house on Cloet Street, none of her jewellery was costume or paste, and though her weekly column brought in only a moderate salary there was never any talk of being stretched. I could stop at a cash machine and make a withdrawal, but this would create obvious problems later. If The Agency accepted cards I would be able to go into the personal savings that I kept separate from the joint account and used for birthdays. But then there would be a record. I tried to anticipate an appropriate sum, but it was impossible. As much as a year's worth of dental insurance for the family? A holiday, or a second-hand car? I had no idea what such a service cost. Heat bloomed through me and I felt suddenly nauseous. Aside from everything else, the thought of paying out hundreds of pounds without John's knowledge made my hands weak.

I lowered the window an inch or two, and took a deep breath. Air buffeted into the car. It was cool and damp, and brought with it the tarry smell of the road. The wind was getting worse, and the brake lights of wagons in the inside lane began to flash on and off. A few heavy raindrops hit the windscreen, and then it began to shower. I slowed down. There was no rush. Volleys of leaves flew across the carriageway and stuck under the wiper blades. I imagined myself caught by a strong gust, losing control of the car, ploughing through the central reservation and across the oncoming lanes. I imagined them finding me, hanging inside a cage of crumpled metal, slack-necked and bleeding over the dark red suit. The family would not know why I had been going into the city, dressed as I was. I thought of John's face, stricken, his fingers pinching his hips, trying hard not to break down, just as he had at his mother's funeral before collapsing into grief. And an old memory came too, of the night John and I had met, our first time in an upstairs room full of coats, the music of the party below like another layer between the world and us, his face contorted as he moved, his hand gripping my throat, the rawness, and his breathless incapacitation when it was over. There had been a fierceness in the beginning, before we really knew each other, before we settled into our tender, more considerate patterns. I saw myself in those early years, holding the railings of the headboard, braced, pushing against him, fighting for control of the space we were using. I saw John, pinning my arms down, his vast movements, the sheets pushed outwards and outwards like a ruined form. It was suddenly clear to me that this was madness. What I was doing could not possibly go unmarked. Surely some slip, some twist of fate, would give me away, and it would be impossible to explain. There was no explanation. Even I did not understand what I was doing.

I glanced in the rear-view mirror, indicated, and pulled over onto the hard shoulder. I took my hands off the steering wheel, squeezed them into fists and shook them. Wagons rumbled alongside the car, spraying the windscreen. Tailwinds made the car shudder. I glanced at the dashboard clock. It was nine forty-five. There was still time to think, time to reconsider. I took a familiar CD from the glove box, inserted it into the player and the first track began.

I had been married for fourteen years. There had been no crimes committed on either side. There was so little to regret. But in the end, thinking of our life together made no difference. It was as if love had become scentless, bloodless, it had somehow lost its vitality. I put the car into gear, waited for a gap in the traffic and pulled away.

The Agency

*

After navigating the unfamiliar road system, I found a car park near The Agency's address. The building was on a quiet street. Its façade was unremarkable: three-storey, Edwardian, pale brick, like most of the others in the row. The door was heavy and black and looked newly painted, its lustre like liquorice. There was a brass plaque chased into the masonry with an engraved street number, and above that a bell and an intercom. There was no name, nor the name of any other company listed in the building. It looked like an ordinary corporate town house, containing any number of nondescript offices. I walked away, waited for a few minutes nearby, ridiculously holding my phone to my ear. No one entered or left the building. I walked the length of the street, looking up at the corners of the end buildings, and then I walked back and rang the bell. Almost immediately a buzzer sounded inside and I heard a heavy mechanical *click*. I pushed open the door, turned to look at the empty street, and quickly entered.

Inside the passageway there was a polished wooden side table and a painted glass lamp. The walls were eggshell-coloured. There was silence until a vehicle drove past on the road outside, its engine muffled. My heart was tapping behind my breastbone. A bitter taste had risen in my mouth and I wished I had not drunk so much coffee before leaving the house. Ahead, at the end of the passageway, stood an elegant staircase with spiralled iron rods and an exquisite curving balustrade. I was about to move and go up it when a door to my right opened. A young dark-haired man in a suit came out. He extended his hand.

Hannah? You found us alright?

I nodded, took his hand, and he placed his other gently on the back of my wrist.

Yes, thank you.

He nodded. Of course. I'm Alistair. We spoke on the phone. Let's go into the office, shall we? That's a beautiful suit. Westwood?

He had a soft, burred accent, Scottish, perhaps pared from the Highlands. He held the door for me and I entered the room.

There was a large cast-iron fireplace with decorative tiles and trivets. A vase of white stargazers stood on the mantel. A desk was pushed against the far wall; on top were a slim white laptop and the intercom hub. An armchair and a sofa faced each other across a low table. The carpet was Regency blue, and the room had been wallpapered in a pale green period design. It was a richer interior than the passageway, and smelled newly cleaned. The young man waited for me to catch his eye and then he spoke.

OK. First things first, welcome to The Agency. Thank you for coming.

There was a pause, and then he asked, Would you like a coffee? I shook my head. He brought his hands together in front of his chest, the fingertips steepled. It was a demure gesture, or it was artful; either way he seemed too young for such mannerisms.

Tea? A glass of champagne, perhaps?

He smiled and raised his eyebrows. I could feel a tiny muscle pulsing under my eye.

Oh, champagne! he said quickly. It's practically the afternoon, isn't it? Please, sit.

He moved to a side door and opened it. There was a small kitchen beyond; the corner of a refrigerator was visible and a cabinet door. I heard the dinging of glassware, a muted pop, and the wet crackle of the drink being poured. Alistair reappeared holding two tall stems. He set them on the table, sat down on the couch and held out a hand.

Join me?

The leather of the chair clucked and sighed as I sat.

I'm sorry, I said. I was referred by a friend and

it's all very new to me. I suppose I don't really know what I'm doing or what I should do. I think I haven't completely made up my mind, about anything. I'm sorry.

Alistair smiled again. His teeth were crowded, but white.

Please don't apologise. It's wonderful that you found us, even just as an option. Here.

He reached forward and slid the stem towards me. I lifted it to show willing, and then looked at him properly. He was clean-faced, with a remarkably good complexion, and his hair had been cut to fall one side of his brow in a sharp, stylish way. There was a classic, vintage tailoring to his suit, and he wore the waistcoat buttoned. He would not have been out of place in a pre-war television drama. He had obviously been created to go with the location, though his attentiveness and etiquette seemed unforced. He was attractive in a singular and imperfect way. Is this what women want? I thought. I took a sip. The champagne tingled against my lip, and was crisp and sour. I knew I would drink it too quickly if I kept it in my hand, so I set it back on the table.

Thank you, I said, and again he replied, Of course.

He leaned back against the upholstery and crossed his legs.

So, Hannah. Really The Agency prefers to consider this initial meeting as you interviewing us. We absolutely hope to be able to provide you with everything you'd wish, but it's entirely at your discretion, whether you think we're suitable for you, and whether you choose to engage us. We're versatile, and we operate a legal service, on and off the premises, but we understand that some special requirements also need to be met.

He paused a moment, as if to allow time for the words, and their meaning, to be metabolised.

We want to meet all possible needs. So it's best to be as specific as possible in these early stages. He uncrossed his legs and leaned forward. There was a sheet of paper on the table. He drew it towards him and lifted a corner.

Hannah. Would it be very boring if I offered you some literature, so you can get a sense of what we provide, and we can get a sense of what you prefer?

I was watching his mouth as he spoke. He was moderating his language, his politeness had escalated, and his lips were amplifying the shapes they made.

I'll let you have some privacy while you look through. There's no time pressure at all. Often people like to consider things *at home* again before committing to a further appointment.

The last phrase had been cleverly chosen. He had been cleverly chosen. The calibration was perfect. He slid the sheet of paper towards me, took a pen from his inside pocket and set it on the table.

Please don't worry. This is simply to help us identify your preferences. You can take it away after we're done. We don't keep any records here.

He pressed his hands together again and stood.

I'll leave you to it. There's a call button on the desk when you're done. Don't forget your champagne.

I took another sip, aware that for all his deference, I was being gently marshalled. There was something deliberately neutral about the meeting, but the young man standing over me was passively steering things. Alistair had been selected for his social skills and his intelligence. Or was the enterprise his, I wondered. Had he recognised a niche in the market and filled it? How old was he? In his mid-twenties? Only a few years ago he might have been one of John's Politics students. He moved towards the door.

Oh, and Hannah? he said quietly. I should just make it clear, the first question, gender, doesn't apply to you. We know you're female. All our members are, as you're probably aware.

He smiled. The door closed.

I felt as if I'd been holding my breath for the entire

discussion. I blew air out, reached for the glass and drank to the halfway mark. Alistair's glass had not been touched and it occurred to me that it had actually been poured and left for me as well, to make the proceedings as comfortable as possible. I stood and went over to the fireplace. The inlaid tiles were Arts and Crafts. The lilies on the mantel were real. Their scent was delicate, elative. The petals were austerely white, but here and there were orange pollen stains. The stamens had not been removed and on their tips were gathered beads of sap. It was not just nerves or caffeine making me edgy, exciting me. I did not feel unsafe or exposed, as I had supposed I would. I knew that I could leave, easily, and without drama, while the reception room was empty. Alistair would not be surprised to find me gone when he came back. But I didn't want to leave. And I knew he also would not be surprised to find me still there.

I sat back down on the warm leather and picked up the sheet of paper. It was a form with a series of boxes to tick, not unlike the questionnaires found in beauty clinics. I scanned through. The term used was *companion*. There was brevity to the phrasing, options that I had perhaps anticipated, but some of the later choices were startling. *Film, Restraints, Doll, Defecation.*

Anthea had not gone into detail about her experiences. I tried to guess how she might have navigated the form, how straightforward or strange her choices. My life seemed so simple. I did not think what I wanted was unusual. I picked up the pen and struck a line through the appropriate boxes. Then I selected two more from the last section. I finished the champagne, went to the desk and pressed the call bell.

Alistair knocked and opened the door, greeting me warmly, as if we were old friends. He had removed his suit jacket. Underneath was a fashionably striped shirt. The waistcoat was still buttoned.

OK, Hannah. If you would like me to review the form now, and if you're happy for me to arrange an introduction, I most certainly can. Otherwise I can get in touch with you in a few days with a referral and a telephone number. Would you like me to top you up there?

He gestured to my empty glass. I shook my head.

I have to drive, but thank you.

There was a pause. I expected him to say it again, 'Of course', but he did not. The veneer of professionalism remained but now I felt his keener interest. It was not flirtation, the way he was looking at me, but curiosity perhaps, as to my proclivities. The atmosphere in the room felt low, as if the wind outside had relieved the room of its currents. I held the sheet of paper out. My hand was steady. If Alistair noticed the change he gave no indication. He sat opposite me again, crossed his legs, and read through the profile. His eyes flickered across the page, he nodded once, but his face remained expressionless. I tried to guess his age again. Old enough to front such a business and be intuitive. Young enough to seem coltish and, when necessary, submissive. How many wives had he hosted in this room? How much power did he hold? There was obviously money and experience behind the venture, though surely not his. However entrepreneurial he was, however philogynous, he could not be so knowing. Suddenly I was certain he had not orchestrated the enterprise. No. He was skilled, but he was, in effect, a drone. The Agency had been conceived by a woman. The rooms, the tidy gatekeeper, the subtle game; it all belonged to a woman.

After a minute Alistair looked up and smiled.

Hannah, there's a lounge upstairs that's very comfortable. It's free at the moment. Would it be convenient for you to wait ten minutes or so, while I make a quick phone call? That outfit really is beautiful.

*

When I arrived home it was getting dark. I checked my emails, put a load of laundry into the machine and ran a bath. In the bedroom I took off the suit, covered it with the plastic sleeve and hung it up in the wardrobe. I sat on the edge of the bed and removed my shoes. I turned them over. There was slight scuffing on the soles, nothing more than if they'd been trodden across the gravel path outside the house to break them in. A ladder ran through one of my stockings, following its black seam. I unhooked the clasp and rolled the material down my leg, then took off the other. A bruise was spreading under my hip bone. If he noticed, I would tell John that the car door had swung shut against it in the wind. The marks around my wrists I would have to cover until they faded. I put the stockings back in their packet, took them to the rubbish bin in the kitchen and placed them underneath the topmost items. I reached inside the plastic drum and pushed the waste matter further down towards the bottom, then emptied a half-eaten container of yogurt over everything. I washed my hands, poured a glass of water and went back upstairs.

My skin felt tender as I climbed into the bath. I took my hair down, lay back against the enamel and closed my eyes. I could still see the patterns in the green wallpaper at The Agency and the elaborate wrought-iron rosettes in the banister of the staircase. Those dripping orchids. I could see the interior of the cab that had driven me through the wet, leaf-strewn streets. The hotel foyer and the number of the room. The black petals of the brooch pinned to my burgundy jacket, and the jacket lying in a dark pool of material on the floor. He was not exact, not as I had imagined. He had asked for a phrase, to stop everything, and I had given John's mother's name, Alexandra, but it had not been used.

After half an hour in the bath I felt loose and hot, as if I were beginning to come apart, as if I was as smooth as the water. I stood up, pulled the plug out and turned the shower to a cool setting. When I had dried myself and dressed I went into the lounge to clear up the children's mess. Jamie's school jumper was stuffed behind the settee, there were magazines and books scattered about, a sweet stuck in the fibres of the rug. It was too late to think about work, so I shut the computer down. In the hallway my bag was open and inside it I could see the blue light on my phone flashing. There were three missed calls. The first was from John, saying he would be home about seven with Katie after her swimming lesson. The second was from Alistair, confirming my next appointment. I deleted both after listening. The last message was from Anthea King, asking if I could mind her daughter after school the following day. A note of distraction sounded in her voice, and I heard the rattle of the keyboard as she typed something. The message ended. I called her back and agreed to mind Laura. We spoke for a moment or two. There was a pause in the conversation, and then came her gay, indecorous laughter.

Oh, we must catch up soon. I do hope you had a jolly time in the city today.

I was just visiting a relative, I said.

She laughed again. Yes. Of course, darling. Of course.

She Murdered Mortal He

When the fight was over she left the salon tent and walked towards the beach. The way through the jungle was signposted. It was not yet dark. She was not sure what to do. Everything was out of control. She wanted to think clearly, get her bearings. She wanted not to feel so lost, or to feel so lost that nothing more could be taken. Mostly she just wanted to leave their room. She followed the path through the bowed and necking trees. The air was heavy, greenly perfumed, and the avian calls were loud and greasy. The dust felt cool against her feet. She turned left, then right. They had walked this way earlier, after arriving in the complex, to get to the town a mile up the coast, and they'd been surprised by the sudden vertiginous drop. The jungle ended abruptly and the dunes were incredibly steep. There was no gradation. The dark canopy, with its humidity and silicone music, gave way to a long corrugated ramp, ionic sea wind, vast space – two utterly different realms. The path wove through the brush. She stooped under low branches, careful, despite the surging recklessness, where she trod, not wanting to disturb snakes coiled under the leaves.

What's wrong, she had asked him, as they lay on the bed after their trip into town, stroking his back. You seem distracted.

Nothing, he had said a few times.

But she had persisted. What? What is it?

After a while he had turned.

Something feels different, he had said. Don't you think so?

They had been together a year. He had said nothing like this before. She had knelt upright at the corner of the bed, and put her arms round herself. He had begun breathing hard, blowing out, as if what he was saying, or was about to say, was heavy labour.

Something feels wrong between us. We should talk about it.

Then, with such terrible ease, it had all begun to unravel. Their meeting at the Hallowe'en party, and his ridiculous bloody stump. Their conversation about Flaubert, the shared cigarette. The kiss, in his terrible heatless flat. The late-night texts. Their first dinner party with its triumphant co-concocted fish soup. The formative moments, winding away, as if they had never been safe.

She picked her way through the foliage, through

muggy, scented chambers. Now the birds around her sounded electrical, like mobile phones. Every time she heard a melodic stammer she thought she would come upon someone talking. But there was no one on the path – the lodge was almost deserted, the other salon tents were empty. And there was no phone signal here. An occasional bar crept up on the display, then disappeared, a faint or false satellite. She stopped. All around were intimately knotted branches. The pulp inside the peeling bark was an extraordinary garish orange. There were leopards in here, they had been told by their driver – elusive, flaxen-eyed creatures that were almost never seen. Or seen too late. They were gradually coming back after years of being hunted. And the thought occurred to her, that if one of them were to take her now, powerfully by the neck, and drag her up into the crux of a tree, what then? Nothing then. She began walking again.

*

The tide was on the way out. She knew this even before coming upon the beach. She could hear its retreat, the sonorous hiss at the back of its throat. The trees finished. The air thinned. She saw the ocean for the second time that day, and drew a breath. How had she forgotten its scale, its grandeur? The water was a literal blue. All blues. For a moment the scene looked like one of the cheap plasticised paintings of the Mediterranean on sale in the harbours of southern Europe. But this was not the Mediterranean. This was a body of water so prodigious it looked almost solid, except for the ragged crests, the series of spraying breakers that came from far out and swept up the shore, driving sand high into the jungle. This ocean generated its own wind. It bellowed. Its inhabitants were huge breaching creatures that were of no consequence. After an aborted attempt earlier that day they had not swum. Even knee-deep the undertow had been too strong, dragging their feet down into trenches, making them flap their arms, squat forward and wade against the pull.

The holiday had been her idea. She had read an article in the travel section of the *Guardian*. The writer had urged people to come before the character of the place changed irreversibly. She'd pitched the idea, of being more intrepid, of a different kind of trip, and after a week or two he'd agreed. They had left the hire car at the South African border and been brought to the tiny, fledgling resort in an old white Land Rover with an insecure driver's door that kept swinging open. The driver's name was Breck. He was from Richards Bay, but had come north because the opportunities for new tourism were exciting. He taught scuba and arranged whale-watching during migration season. As he drove down the unmade roads he waved to the women carrying canisters and baskets on their hips and heads, and to the children. There were children everywhere. When they passed a man with no hands sitting on an oil drum he said, Look. Long sleeves, I reckon. He's from Zimbabwe. A few have come here. It used to be the other way round. What do you do? he'd asked them.

I'm a lawyer.

Ah. Right. Clever guy. And you?

I manage a company that arranges ghost tours.

Oh, what, to see ghosts?

Places where people have seen ghosts, in London. There are lots of places.

But not the ghosts?

No.

That's good. Then they can't ask for their money back.

Not really, no.

Though an American woman had fainted in Whitechapel the previous week and had made an official complaint. She had not realised the tour would include spots where victims of the Ripper had been found, she said. She just wanted to see queens and princes. Breck had worked hard to sell the area to them, playing up the economic recovery, making claims about the restoration of wildlife.

The transit vehicle needed to be booked in advance. The border checkpoint closed at 5 p.m. Though she did not want to stay at the lodge that night, though she could not face seeing him after what had been said, or half said, her window to leave was gone.

She waded down the steep sand bank, leaning back, sinking up to her calves. The beach levelled off and she began to walk towards the headland with the cliff path that could be taken into town. Crabs were working the tideline, scissoring pieces of blue jellyfish, dragging the dissections backwards into their burrows. The sun was setting on the other side of the dunes. She could not see any red display, just a dull luminescence above the treetops. She turned and looked behind. The beach was misty with spray and deserted, a long alluvial corridor. He was not following. He would not follow; she knew that. She had refused to let him comfort her after she'd begun crying. He would adhere to this preference, even if she did not.

She continued on. She replayed the argument in her head, accurately or inaccurately; it did not matter. By the end of the conversation a reptilian dullness had crept into his eyes. It was as if he was persuading himself of his own point of view, of mutual failure.

I used to think you were strange and amazing, he had said. But I wonder how much we have in common. We seem to want different things. Why are we here?

She had stopped crying now, and did not feel sick with panic any more. She felt tender and very alert, as if having risen from a fever, as if driving a new body. There was the reek of kelp all about. Though she was profoundly alone, she felt self-conscious. Observed. To her left, at the top of the rise, the jungle was greenish-brown, oily and complicated, immune to the salt air. It was like a mouth, or many mouths, spitting out the sand that it was relentlessly fed. Now that she was looking up at it, the entity seemed superior to the ocean. The uppermost branches shifted and rustled. Nothing flew above. Nothing flitted in or out. Everything inside was hidden. What was he doing back in their room, she wondered. Repacking his bag, perhaps? Reading a book? Or maybe he was asleep; oblivious to everything, making use of that shut-off mechanism men could rely upon in such situations.

She walked on. The ocean wind was strong. Grains of airborne sand stung her arms and face. Her dress fluttered. Perhaps he was right. Perhaps they were not in step. Why had she wanted to come here, to a place like this, with its memory of recent troubles? Sub-Saharan gothic, he had joked, a busman's holiday. He had booked two weeks off work, which meant handing an important case over to a colleague. They had flown into Johannesburg, visited a few game parks, photographed giraffe and zebra, then come north. They had arrived at midday and the staff had been friendly. The receptionist had kissed them both three times. They had lain on towels and applied sun-lotion, and had eaten lunch in a cafe in town. They had talked about going up to the ruined lighthouse on the highest dune to see the sunset. But the sense of this being a holiday was somehow absent. There were still signs of the war – abandoned farms, ruins. Now, separate from him, any meaningful frame for being here was gone. She was anomic. The sand was difficult to tread. Her ankle kept turning. She began to feel foolish.

After a while she turned and looked behind again. There was a white form a few hundred metres back down the beach, where the path to the lodge began. His white linen shirt. Briefly, a sense of elation possessed her. He was looking for her, which meant he was worried. It meant a reversal, perhaps. Should she wait for him or walk on and let him make up the distance? Should she make it easy? She lingered a moment. No. This was his doing. He had instigated their division. He would have to catch up with her. She turned and walked on, not with haste, but purposefully, her steps widening over the dry reefs, the flats of her sandals slapping the soles of her feet. Crabs scattered towards the water. She went about thirty paces. Then she slowed. Perhaps he would not see her so far away. Her dress was pale; she might be indistinguishable against the sand. And she did want to be seen, didn't she? She paused, looked behind again. The white shape was in the same position, perhaps a little closer. She squinted. The surf was creating an illusory fog; the light was thickening. It was difficult to gain focus. She bridged her hands over her eyes.

The shape was low to the ground, and was not particularly large, not elongated like a man. It was not him. Her disappointment was simply confirmation. She knew he would not come. Still, she was annoyed to have hoped, to have permitted the minor fantasy. The white object was not large, but it was too big to be a seabird. Something mid-sized, then. It was definitely moving; it had velocity, a gait, but she could not tell in which direction it was heading, towards her or away. She peered along the corridor of sand. Towards her. It was coming towards her. She could make out a rocking motion, forwards and backwards, side to side. A creature loping, or running. A spark of alarm fired across her chest. Suddenly there was no air to breathe, though the beach was a cathedral of air. She stood still, lifted a hand to her mouth. A creature running towards her. A creature running towards her. She couldn't move, couldn't make a clear assessment.

There were many dangers here; all outlined in the literature she had received from her health centre. Since arriving on the continent she had retained a prudent fear of the environment. The disease. The bacteria. The wildlife. Not all of it could be washed away, contained, or immunised against. On the way to one of the game parks they had passed an iron-roofed clinic. Outside there had been a long queue of patients. A white doctor was leaning against the clinic wall taking enormous rushed bites out of a sandwich. On the road to the border the traffic had suddenly stopped. After a minute or two the cars ahead had pulled away and driven on, cautiously. A rhino was on the carriageway. It was grazing unspectacularly on the verge as they crawled past. Its plated torso was earth-coloured. Its eye was a tiny dark recess. Twenty miles later they had passed a woman in the middle of the road, waving her arms up and down. Then they'd seen the body, splayed, folded over itself, made boneless by the impact. A young man, walking to work, perhaps. The debris of his briefcase lay in the oncoming lane.

It was everywhere, close to the surface, or rupturing through.

She turned and walked on, quicker than before. She lengthened her stride. Whatever was behind her might simply have strayed onto the beach, and would cut up into the brush again, leaving her alone. If it was following without motive, or through curiosity, she could probably make it to the headland pass before it came too close. Just walk, she thought. Walk. Don't run.

The drifts were hard going. The dry crust seemed to support her whole weight for a moment then became slack and collapsed and her heels submerged. Sand worked its way between her toes. She walked closer to the shoreline, where the ground was firmer and less abrasive, but still her feet seemed poorly designed for the task. They were narrow, hoof-like. Her shins ached. The glow on the other side of the trees was fading. Soon even the dusk light would be extinguished. There were no long twilights like at home. Here the shift came swiftly. She walked on. The crabs scuttled away as she approached, or circled about her feet, their claws held aloft. She did not want to look behind again. Nor did she want to imagine what was there. The latter option was worse. The dress she was wearing was low-backed. Her flesh felt exposed. She was all meat, all scent. Had whatever it was gained? Had it materialised properly? A thing born from the jungle: acute and mindless in its predation, glistening-jawed. Her nails dug into her palms as she paced. It might be a breath away from her. Or it might be gone. Turn, she thought. Turn now.

She stopped and turned and the white shape was coming faster, on all fours. A clean bolt of panic struck against her sternum. She wheeled round. Not far ahead volcanic cliffs rose and an uneven stage of rocks began. She began to run; heavy, stumbling steps. It would be the only way she could make the headland, so she could clamber up to a higher, safer place. But it was like running in a dream. The turgid ground, the dreadful incapacity. She pulled herself forward. She fought the sand. Her thighs burnt, began to seize. Stop, she thought. You have to stop. Showing fear means accepting you are prey. She stopped. She turned and looked back.

It was a dog. A big white dog was coming after her; paws skimming the sand, head held low. It was tracking her. It was engaged in the act, but not at full speed, not in pursuit. She drew herself in, filled her lungs. OK. A dog. A dog was not the worst possibility, even if wild. She'd had the shots, painfully and expensively in the upper arm, there was still a hard lump under the surface, as if a coin had been inserted. And she could recall no reports in the news of tourists set upon and killed by dogs; such a thing must be uncommon. It was war or malaria or road accidents that spawned tragedy. Though she could recall now, luridly, and out of nowhere, the face of that little girl from the north-east, from Sunderland, who had been mauled by the family bull terrier earlier in the year. She could recall her face and neck in the photographs: a grotesque map of welts, flaps and bruises, crescents of black stitches. Then the later pictures: her skull bone grafted over, her nose rebuilt, less striking, surgical disfigurements.

She put her shoulders back, stood her ground, waited for the thing to catch up. When it was within close range the dog lifted its head and veered to the side, then came into line with her, higher up on the ramp of sand. It stopped. The dog looked down at her. Its eyes were dark, bright. Big paws. It was part Labrador, perhaps, blunt-headed, its fur dirty. There was no collar. Its tongue spooned from its jaw. It looked at her. Its eyes were very, very bright. Under the muddy coat was a distended belly and long black teats. It did not appear emaciated.

She was not usually afraid of dogs. She had had a dog as a child.

Come here, she said. Come. Come here.

The dog dropped its head and came and stood next to her, its warm body pressing against her leg. She put out a hand and let it sniff between her fingers, then she stroked its head, carefully. The fur was damp and gummy. There were lumps on the ears. A stray. But it had once been tame, and it was still tame. Not wild. Not rabid. Biddable. The relief was like stepping into a warm bath. Something within her let go. Her muscles relaxed. She began crying again, though gently, not as she had after the fight. The dog nudged her hand with its head. She petted the dog with the tips of her fingers, combing the sticky fur. It continued to lean warmly against her leg. After a minute she wiped her eyes and walked on again. The dog held back for a moment then followed and fell in beside her.

You gave me a scare, she said. Listen, I'm not going to keep you.

She continued down the beach with the dog as her companion. She walked slowly. Now and then the dog brushed past and went ahead, then came back to her side. A couple of times it chased after crabs, bounding towards them, knocking clods of wet sand up with its paws and snapping at the angry, fencing creatures. Then it came to her side again, as if demonstrating obedience.

You know where you're going? she asked. Well, you seem to.

She watched the dog. It was nice to watch. It moved deliberately, in accordance with its proclivities. It sniffed seaweed and chased crabs. Then it wanted to be at her side. For no real reason its presence made her feel better. At the headland rocks they both paused and then picked their way along the puddled outcrop. There were pools the shape of hexagons, strange geological structures. At the edge of the headland the ocean washed over them. As they began to round the cliff, the jungle disappeared from sight. The dog stepped through the shallower pools. It lapped some of the water.

Hey, don't drink that.

She thought perhaps the dog would not come up the cliff path but as she began the ascent it followed, bounding up off its back legs onto the boulders. It squeezed past her where the path was almost too narrow for them both, then wanted to lead. The dog trotted ahead confidently, piloting. Perhaps it belonged to someone in the town, she thought, and had just ranged out. In places she had to bend and scrape through bushes. She brushed her shoulders down afterwards, shook out her dress. The rock was volcanic, sculpted into minuscule peaks. Not far below the ocean hawked in and out of eroded gullies. With the sun off it, the water was no longer the intense blue, but colourless.

It took five minutes to round the headland, and then the settlement came into view, the green-roofed cabins on stilts, thatched huts, the seafood bar, and the little blue Portuguese church with its naive Madonna painted on the gable, her figure and head undulating like an expressionist portrait. There were steps carved into the rocks. She walked down them with the dog and walked along the bay to the launching stage, past a few fishermen who nodded at her, and when she arrived at the edge of the town she stopped.

OK. Go home, she said to the dog. Go on.

The dog sat and faced her. Its teats hung from its black belly. Its claws were long and curved and the webs between looked sore. It cocked its head and looked as if it did not understand the command, or as if she might issue another, preferable instruction. In the failing light its eyes were huge. She made her tone firmer.

Go home. Go. Home.

She clapped her hands in front of its face. The dog got to its feet but did not move. She turned her back and walked away. She glanced back. The dog was not following. It was standing in the same spot on the beach, its ears knuckled upwards, watching her. She continued to walk. When she looked back properly the dog was trotting down to the edge of the water, chasing crabs again.

*

She did not really know what she was doing, coming into the town. Acting out of anger, but her anger had ebbed now. Though she knew it was relatively safe – Breck, the driver, had vouched for that – she was nervous. She did not want to go back yet. She could not bear the idea of taking up where they had left off. She could not bear seeing him in an altered state, unmoved by her, his eyes blank. She wanted to sit and have a drink, sit and think. She had to get her mind round the situation, had to assimilate it. She'd probably be able to get a ride back to the lodge complex later; locals seemed amenable to casual work. Or she could walk back along the beach. It would be a clear night by the look of the sky. Let him wonder where she had gone. Let him think about things too, what it was he had said, or tried to say, what it was he might be giving up. He was as trapped here as she was, at least until tomorrow when the Land Rover could be booked. If there was a lover he had not yet admitted to – and she had asked, she had demanded to know – he would not be able to reach her by phone to say, yes, he had begun to break things off. No more than she could reach a friend, or member of her family, to be consoled.

She still did not really understand what was going on. He had said nothing about feeling unhappy previously. Why had she asked him, again and again, what was wrong, instead of taking a nap with him on the bed before dinner? Had her asking created a situation that would not otherwise have existed? If she had not asked him, if she had rested her cheek on his back and her hand on his stomach, and had slept for an hour against his side, would the argument never have taken place? Would they still be together? They had had sex that morning, in a different bed, in a game lodge further south. The sex had been good; he had initiated it, and when she had taken him into her mouth he had said her name with surprise, as if at a loss, as if helpless, and he had been desperate to be inside her and they had both moved well, automatically, uniformly, and when she had come he had too. He had seemed moved, looking down at her. Did he know then that later in the day he would be saying such damaging things?

What about this morning, she had said during the argument. You felt something for me then, didn't you?

Yes, he said, something. But that's unfair. It's different. Sex is not rational.

They had bickered on the drive up, about nothing important, when to make a rest-stop, whether to buy more bottled water. They had disagreed about whether tourism was a good or bad thing for countries such as this. But the true argument had seemingly come out of nowhere. As if with her arch invitation to speak his mind, she had conjured from a void the means to destroy everything. As if he had suddenly decided it could end. Like deciding he wanted her phone number. Like deciding to get a spare door key cut for her. How easily inverted the world could be. How dual it was.

She made her way along the dirt road towards the cafe. Lights outside the bars were coming on. The evening was still warm. People were sitting drinking beer on the concrete groyne. Three surfers were loading their boards into rusting pick-up trucks. There were locals still trying to sell cashews and carvings. The last of the vendors watched her as she passed by but did not approach. Earlier that day they had made good pitches to them both as they lay on towels reading.

Buy these nuts; they are delicious. Just try one for free and then decide.

Perhaps they could witness the recent distress in her, like looking at a dishevelled tract of land a storm has lately passed through. She walked past the oil drum where the handless man had been sitting. She went into the cafe that they had been in earlier, feeling safer for the vague familiarity. She sat at an empty table and the same waiter approached her, a young man, in his twenties, wearing a yellow and green T-shirt.

Hello again.

Hello.

He greeted her pleasantly, but she could see that he was confused. He kept looking at the door. This was not a resort, if it could yet be called a resort –

locked in by sand roads, and visited by only a few dozen tourists a week – where a woman would drink alone. She had three hundred rand in the pocket of her dress. She ordered a beer. The waiter nodded and went to the refrigerator and brought one over. He set it down on the table with great care, positioning a glass next to the bottle. She thanked him.

Obrigada.

And to eat?

She shook her head. He nodded and withdrew.

She sipped the beer. She thought about him, and what her life might be like without him. They lived in the same city and saw each other regularly, socialised with each other's friends. Most nights they spent to-gether. They had taken a few trips. This was the most exotic – a twelve-hour flight, prophylaxis and rehyd-ration tablets. They had been getting along fine, she thought. She tried to find any recent tells. Perhaps he had been moody these past few weeks, a little in-different, stressed at work. He had been curt with her when she said, again, that she wanted to change jobs, that the tours were not what she really wanted to do. But nothing had seemed worrying. She was thirty-one. The thought of going back out, on dates, to parties and clubs, looking for someone, having to generate that intellectual and sexual optimism, made her feel tired. She remembered their first night to-gether. He had taken her for a walk in the park by his house, and out for dinner. They had undressed in the living room of his cold flat and had moved to the bedroom only when his flatmate's door had opened. They had barely slept. They were astonished by each other. The next day they had eaten a late breakfast, gone to the cinema, and come back to the flat to collect her necklace. They had had sex again, better, quick and inconsiderate, her underwear taken off, her skirt left on, and then she had gone to work. She had felt extreme happiness. There had been nothing to lose.

She finished the beer and ordered another. The waiter's politeness increased as he took her order. She knew she was making him nervous. But she wanted the anaesthesia, the insulation. She wanted to go back and not to care about losing him. Part of her thought she should stay out, stubbornly, sleep on the beach, or try to make other arrangements, but she did not have the resolve. She had been gone a few hours; that was enough. If it was over, it was over. She took a few more sips, then pushed the bottle away. She put the rand on the table and stood and left the bar.

OK, the waiter called after her. OK. OK, now.

She felt soft at the edges as she moved, and lesser. Outside the sky was dark, full of different stars. The world seemed overturned but balanced.

A few men called out to her as she walked back towards the beach, not in a threatening way. She did not understand the language and it did not matter what they said. The worst had already happened tonight. In a way she was immune, even from the chill that was beginning. She walked along the beach. It was easier to walk when she felt soft. She was more flexible, more adaptable. There was a quarter moon, brilliantly cut. She could see the shape of the headland and the pale drape of sand leading up to it. The tide had receded. The waves sounded smaller. The crests looked thinner. She could probably walk around the lower section of the cliff now. Beneath everything disastrous, everything menacing, there was honesty. It was beautiful here. She had known it would be. Perhaps that's why she had wanted to come.

As she was walking something loomed up at her side and pushed against her leg. She flinched and stopped moving, then relaxed.

You again.

She petted the dog's head.

Have you been waiting? Look, you're not mine.

The dog was leaning against her, warmly, familiarly. Its coat in the near darkness seemed cleansed. The dog pressed against her and she put a hand on its back. She had avoided touching it properly before, worried about grime and germs. Now she crouched down and took hold of the dog's ears, then under its jaw, and rubbed.

Is that nice?

There was a fusty smell to the animal. The muzzle was wet and when she lifted it up to look underneath she could see it was dark and shiny.

Hey. What have you had your face in, stupid?

Something viscous and warm. When she took her hands away they were tacky. She knew, before the thought really registered, that it was blood.

Oh no, she said. What have you done? What have you done to yourself?

The dog shook its head. Its jowls slopped about. She wiped her face on her inner arm. Perhaps it had gone off and fought with another dog over some scraps while she was in the bar. Or one of the crabs it had been chasing had pinched it. She took hold of the dog's head again and moved it around to try to find a wound, but it was too dark to see properly. The animal was compliant, twitching a little but not pulling back from her grip. It did not seem to be in pain.

She stood up and walked to the edge of the water. She took off her sandals and stepped in. A wave came and soaked the hem of her dress. She stumbled, widened her stance. She slapped her thighs and tried to get the dog to come into the surf, but the dog stood on the beach, watching her, and then it began to whine. After a few attempts she came back out.

OK, she said. You're fine. Let's go.

They walked towards the headland and when they reached the rocks they stayed low and began to pick their way around the pools and gullies. This time the dog did not pilot. It kept close, nudging against her legs. When she looked down she could make out a dark smear on her dress. Where the outcrop became more uneven she bent and felt her way using her hands and was careful where she put her feet. The largest waves washed over the apron of rock against her shins. Towards the end of the headland, water was breaking against the base of the cliff. She timed her move and went quickly, stepping across the geometric stones. A wave came in and she heard it coming and held tightly to the rock face as it dashed upwards, wetting her dress to the waist. She gasped. Her body was forced against the rock. She felt one of her sandals come off. Water exploded around her and rushed away. The haul of the ocean was so great she was sure she'd be taken. She clung to the cliff. Every atom felt dragged. Then the grip released. She lurched around the pillar onto the flat ground, grazing her ankle as she landed. She winced and flexed her foot. She took off the remaining sandal and held it for a moment. Then she threw it away. She wrung out the bottom of her dress. She looked back. The white dog was standing on the other side of the rocky spur, its head hanging low.

Come on, she called. Come on.

It did not move.

Come on, she said. Come on.

The dog stayed on the rocks for a moment and then turned and she could see it was going back the way they had come.

She watched its white body moving. It floated. There seemed to be nothing holding it up. When the shape disappeared she turned and faced the long steep stretch of beach. The ramp of sand disappeared into the black jungle. The white tideline disappeared into the dark body of the ocean. Only the pale boundary was visible. Tideline meeting sand. She began to walk. She could not remember exactly where the hotel path was, about a mile away, but there was a signpost right by it, she knew that. She walked for a long time, feeling nothing but sand grinding the soles of her feet and chafing her ankles, salt tightening on her skin. She prepared herself. She could accept the end now. She could embrace it. No one was irreplaceable. No one. He could go. She would let him go. She did not like his friends, the smug barristers, the university clique, because they did not like her, because she was not their sort. She did not like his reticence or his conservatism, the way he drove, the way he danced. She would miss the sex, the companionship, until she found someone else. And she would find someone else. Let him join the men of the past. Her old lovers were ghosts. None of them had survived; none were missed.

After a while she stopped. She had come too far. She must have missed the let-out. She doubled back and after a time she saw the small skewed signpost at the top of the dune. She leaned forward and climbed up the bank towards it. Sand spilled backwards, skittering down the slope as she moved. Her legs ached. She felt exhausted. All she wanted to do was lie down and sleep. She sat for a moment at the top of the rise and looked at the ocean – a relentless dark mass. Tomorrow she would probably not see it. Then she stood.

*

The entrance of the path was nothing but a void in the jungle. There was still some warmth inside the foliage as she entered. She bent over and felt her way along, through the trees, to the wooden steps and up. She trod carefully. Occasionally she stamped a foot and the noise echoed dully. Under her feet the fine drifts of dust were cold. There was no light, no reflection. She felt invisible. She felt absent. She made her way through the trees, holding her hands out before her and feeling for low-hanging branches. Her eyes adjusted but the darkness continually bled back into their sockets and she had to fight blindness. The birds and the insects were silent. Then, the low-wattage lights of the outer salon tents.

Before she reached the complex she heard aggravated voices. She could not make out the words. She wondered whether he had raised the alarm. She was embarrassed by the thought, by the idea that people might know she had acted rashly, and why. As she came into the clearing where the main lodge was she could see in the external light a group of people standing together. He was not among them. Some of the staff were there, speaking earnestly to each other in Portuguese and an African language. One of them, the woman who had given them their key earlier that day when they checked in, had her arms wrapped around herself and she was rocking slightly. The fuss was embarrassing.

She thought about slipping back to the tent, unseen. She held back for a moment, and then she approached. They turned to look at her. No one spoke. Then the receptionist cried out, came towards her, gripped her painfully by the arms, and looked towards the men.

Ela está aqui! Ela está aqui!

I went for a walk. On the beach.

The woman released her and took a step backwards and raised her hand as if she might be about to strike her. Then she shook her hand and flicked her fingers.

Você não está morta?

I just went for a walk, she said again. What's happening? I'm alright.

There was a period of confusion. The discussion resumed and broke down. The receptionist shook her hands and walked away, into the shadows. She wanted to leave too, go back to the salon tent, face what she must and then sleep, but the intensity of the situation held her. Something was wrong. Her arrival back at the complex had not lessened their distress. One of the men in the group, the sub-manager, stepped forward. He gestured for her to follow.

She walked with him to the entrance of the main lodge. By the doorway, on the ground, there was a bundle of cloths. They were knotted and blood-stained. The man pushed them aside with his foot, into the corner of the wooden porch. She began to feel dizzy. Heat bloomed up her neck.

What is it? she asked. Has there been an accident?

OK, he said. OK. Come inside.

He went through the door. She followed him into the bar and the man gestured for her to sit at a stool and she sat. His face was damp. He was scratching his arm. She heard others from the group entering the bar behind them.

Ah, he said. OK. Your husband. He was looking around for you. He went to find you. He was very worried. He was . . . there was an attack, you see.

He was attacked? By who?

No. Not a fight. We don't really know how it happened. He was found by George one hour ago. Outside, in the dunes. But he was not conscious. There was a lot of blood. The wound is . . .

He called over to the group of men by the door.

Ei, como você diz tendão?

Tendon.

Yes. The bite is in the tendon of his leg. It's very deep. And a lot of blood is gone. Breck is taking him to the hospital. They will probably have to go to Maputo in the ambulance.

She brought her hands to her face.

Oh my God, she said. Oh my God. I didn't think he would come after me.

Her palms smelled musty, like old meat, like a sick animal. She took them away from her mouth and looked up at the man. He was watching her, nervously. His eyes kept flicking away and back towards her, as if she might react dangerously, as if she might faint or bolt. She shook her head.

What was it? Was it a leopard?

No, he said. No. No. There are no leopards.

The Nightlong River

We knew from the November berries what the next months would bring. Everywhere they were hung and clotted in the bushes, ripe and red, like blisters of blood. The hollies came out in autumn, and gave us ideas about selling genuine wreaths at the Hired Lad during Advent, rather than staining ivy with sheep raddle as we'd done in the balder years. Rose hips clung on well past their season, until the birds eventually went with them. The yarrow and rowan hung out their own gaudy bunting. But it was the hawthorn that was the truest messenger that year, for it'd blossomed wildly in May too. The hawthorns sent the hedgerows ruddy as a battle. It meant a full winter of snow. It meant hoar frosts that would stop the hearts of mice in their burrows and harden tree sap under its white grip. The ground would only ever half thaw until spring, like a clod of beef brought from the pantry and moved from cold room to cold room. Flocks would be lost under drifts.

There were other signs that got read too, by the older villagers. The moon's full eclipse in October.

Up along the Solway they said the salmon had run in early, and there was talk of '47, when the fishermen had walked over the frozen sea towards Man with their creels. To whichever quarter a bull faces lying down on All Hallows, from there the wind will blow the better part of winter, the old saying goes. And Sarge Dickinson's Hereford had its withers turned north that day; I saw it as I passed by the paddock holding on to Magda's arm. North. The chill doesn't get crueller in its delivery than direct from the pole. So the berries told us, and we were warned. But they were gorgeous in their prediction too; they lit the back roads with a bright skin-light, even as the first daads dusted the fells, and the becks stiffened, and the feathers of rooks stuck to the walls.

Poor Magda had not been well all year. She'd been ragging too much, as if a week were a month in her Eve's calendar. She had two strange knots under her arms. They felt pliant and downy like wasps' nests when she put my fingers there, saying, Now, Dolly, don't get into a tiz.

And she was weary, weary well past her age. I'd been washing her cloths for her, when she hadn't the strength to soak the cotton herself. She'd no mother or sister to help. Better me than one of the men in the family, I said to her, it was no bother. Her father had taken her to the doctor that summer and nothing came of it for the doctor was unsure of what might cause the condition. A woman's cycle was a mystery at best, he said.

On the second visit he went to his books and an idea came to him that one of the glands in her brain was mis-cooperating. It was working too hard, or something was growing aside it. There were surgeries now to get behind the skull, the doctor informed Magda and her father, for the Great War had sent plenty of the broken-headed to theatre. But the business was full of risk and seldom did the patient intellectually restore. She reported this to me with a smile, sitting against the haystack at the back of Lanty Farrow's barn, where we often met. Her wheaty hair was pinned and tucked away. She had on her old blue bonnet and she knocked against its rim as if on a front door.

Let us in! she said.

To me it seemed so terribly unfair. She was beautiful through her bones, Magda, with her frame as delicately pinched and whittled as a swift's, and barely a swelling on the little wen of her chest. The thought of moving those bones around nigh on broke my heart.

On the third visit it was decided no surgery would be done. The doctor said he hoped things would settle down of their own accord. He talked of primrose oil and vervain, which was strange for a man known to publicly scorn the apothecaries and arsenic peddlers who traded at the sports days with blue bottles and jars. We knew from this the diagnosis was ill. Magda went with his suggestion though, and cut strands of Simpler's Joy from the lonning by her father's cottage.

Hallowed by thou, if thou growest on the ground, she said, as she gathered it up, as if ours was a century older and witches were abroad.

Do you have to be so sinister? I asked.

May as well, she said.

She hung the stinking weeds in the chimney to dry. Her hands became scented with the oil, and the scent set me on edge, for it was a murky perfume, said to attract pigeons and rats as a corpse would, and eels to the resting place of the drowned if it was scattered on water. I took it in mind perhaps her body wanted a husband and was asking too hard, but I didn't say that to her. We'd both avoided it so far. She was my friend and I loved her and there was nothing to be gained by being a turncoat or a hypocrite. Whatever was wrong, it left her with those downy pods and producing as redly as the November hedgerows. I feared for her in a hard winter. All I wanted was to keep her warm.

With the bad news of Magda, the mink had come back to the valley in summer too. We'd been free of them for several years, and were glad of it, and the councils were glad we'd stopped pressing them to admit their presence in the north like a virulent disease, always saying our complaints were for nowt but sooty ghosts. Some village children came back from crawfishing at the river and said they'd seen a black otter, a little one, not paddling the current but riddling up alongside the banks. How did it move, one of the men asked.

Like this, and they undulated their hands up and down. Like a stoaty.

The valley farmers took note, reinforced coops and sheds and cleaned gun barrels, and they waited. August. September.

It wasn't long before we were finding carcasses: first rabbits and moorhens and dippers, then geese, then cats, throats missing, entrails left in piles like evil little votives. There was no thrift to the killing, nothing necessary. A marten or a wildcat will dismantle wire and twine like a patient clockmaker, then steal from the pens and take prey back to the woods. They'll eat all but the bitter gall bladder, so the damage is almost forgivable. But mink, mink are brazen and gluttonous, they're villainous wee devils. They began breaking into the keeps with saw teeth and claws, desecrating everything, tearing up livestock as if it was nothing more than a savage raid. They went through flocks, strew feathers all about. They slaughtered for the slenderest taste of blood seemingly, and the waste was sickening.

When it became clear they would not roam on, and after the bulk of the harvesting was done, the village met up in the church hall. Magda and I sat at the back and listened to them blether and gripe. There would be a hunting party each evening, it was finally decided, for whichever men were available. The pests would be abolished once and for all. However well they'd bred into the territory, every last one would be culled from its riverside lair. *Therefore if thine enemy hunger, feed him; if he thirst, give him drink: for in so doing thou shalt heap coals of fire on his head*, the inscription read above the church hall door. Romans 12.20. But sometimes it's better not to look up. So we began starving the hounds.

*

I didn't know how many mink it would take to make

a cape, but when the idea came to me it didn't recede. A little fur wrap. What better way to keep Magda warm? Magda was as slight as when she'd been a girl, barely filling her own small dresses and her Sunday coat. She'd never grown tall like I had during our school years, and I'd grown used to feeling like a dool trec towering above her. I'd seen mink before. The animals were not much bigger than the span of a griddle plate – the males one rim wider. I estimated it would take no more than eight altogether, using as much of the pelage as could be salvaged, and probably less for the dot of the lass. Two to the elbow, three across the shoulder. Proper insulation for the thin spindle of her body. As I did the morning wash up at the manor, I imagined the dark panels quilting her back and how fine she'd look. The stole would be rough at the joins and the hems, for I was no practised seamstress; my fingers were not the nimblest at such a task. I'd mended my brothers' moleskin breeches when my mother had asked, with her thickest needle and strongest thread, and I'd darned and fixed buttons like any other daughter. It would be a roughish garment like a tinker or poacher's, but I would do my best for Magda this white-hearted winter. I set my mind to the assemblage of vermin.

I rarely hunted. In truth I did not much enjoy it like my brothers, William and Jonah, who went out with the chase every Lady Day and Michaelmas. On occasion I'd been there when they'd baited badgers, but had never felt that gust of excitement when the dogs closed their pack and the jack of their jaws increased. The boys were surprised when I said I'd be coming. Our dogs were unused to smaller quarry, but the bitches were young and I knew they would dig at the banks in a fury when they caught the scent or the sound of a creature down in the earth. The other farmers would not be interested in selling pelts; even together there wouldn't be enough of a quality to bundle up and send to Saville's by way of Carlisle. These were not original Norfolk-bred mink, shiny and sleek and farmed above their natural size. The coasts and moors had worn the wild mink down, dulled its jet fur to caramel. All the parish wanted was to rid the dale of the nuisance and collect up good batches of eggs again.

Doubtless they would have kept the heads for panel trophies. But I made an arrangement with the hunting families. I bartered buttermilk and preserves, the last of our honey, and I lied to old Lanty

Farrow, with his beautiful otter hound and his Winchester, that I'd court his son, Calum. I told them all to shout the dogs off early for the purpose of saving the hides. In the weeks to come I went out in the evening with my brothers and a rifle, the reek of the kennels drifting behind us. Our lanterns hung soft moons over the river and their flames lit the gore of the berries in the briar.

*

November passed by, leaving sleet on the ground and a brown rot to the moors. By the second Sunday of December I had five good pelts. Jonah and William, reading a personal keenness in my presence at the water's edge, agreed to hunt further on downstream, into the next valley. We were an odd threesome, with our coats and our sacks, treading both sides of the river like a Viking party, and lighting damp bonfires between thistles to smoke the devils out. Jonah, who never spoke, would signal for us to pause, signal for us to walk on. The truth of death is a peculiar thing. For there was a fascination to these evenings that went past utility or sport. We were in the hinterlands, a wilding place, where the reign was ours entirely. We were the wolves. We were the lions.

All day I looked forward to treading the banks, with the dogs sooling about in the undergrowth. And the night welcomed me, gave me senses. I was struck by the ability of the river to ferry odours on its back. It seemed to enhance everything it touched: the mineral stones of its bed, the wet shag of the dogs when they went swimming, the bark of sour thorn trees whose roots sipped at the shallows. Sometimes I imagined I could, like the dogs, detect the waft of mink through the ferns. I knew that binary scent of blood's soft iron and glandy secretion. And when an animal blurted from its hole and the dogs took off, or there were pants and whines at the head of a rabbit warren, my heart banged up towards my throat, and my eye focused. As we passed through the twilight territory there were shrills and screeches in the trees – the nocturnal world engaged in its sharp procedures, just as we were.

The lads got used to not looking back every so often to make sure I was keeping up. I managed fine and never complained of the chill against my forehead. I could set the dogs and call them to heel as well as my brothers. I carried our father's leather harrier gloves to hoist up any bodies from between the tails. Twice I shot at mink as they fled, the blunt crack echoing up the fells. In the distance the guns of the Dickinsons and the Harrisons and the Farrows replied. And it was me who eventually shot Tan, the second eldest of our dogs, when she was bitten through her leg and the wound turned septic and she was dying, pity-eyed, unable to stand or take water. Jonah sat inside the house and wept, and his eyes pled, *Dolly, I can't. Will you?*

We hunted clear down to the Eamont, until the current slowed and great sandstone bluffs rose and there was nowhere for the animals to hide or burrow. Of the ones we caught we raised the slack bodies up on forked sticks, dangled them from their necks, like the terrible flags of returning mercenaries. The boys stripped to their waists in the frosty night air and wore mink round their shoulders and paraded home.

*

It was a strange Advent for Magda, this beastly collection. She knew nothing of my plans and probably supposed me to be working extra hours at the estate, saving for a lavender cushion for her gift, or the coral brooch she'd admired in town. While others tied up mistletoe and stirred charms into suet pudding, I set half a dozen mink on the trestle in the woodshed and lopped off their legs and measured out a pattern. They were handsome creatures, but for those evilly slanting bottom fangs. I could see why graceful ladies the country over wanted the full-length affair.

Skin them like a squirrel, my father instructed, and I did so, peeling the fur stiffly backwards as if husking unripe fruit, then scraping away the fat with a Bowie knife. The stripped pink bodies and the heads I left in a heap by the woodshed, where they looked grisly and withered, and I began to feel guilty, as if my mess was equal to that of the dreadful vermin. Eventually I passed them along in a bucket as fodder for the pigs up at High Hullock Howe.

It would have been better to let the pelts air and dry before stitching them together; there were correct treatments I knew this cape would not enjoy in its making, but time was short. The weather was worsening, with two snowfalls in a week and a late Helm Wind off the Pennines, which had left the eastern villages cut off. Magda was confined to her bedroom, cramped and pale. The light in our cottage was poor. I worked early, from seven until nine, as soon as the sun supported any industry, before turning my hand to my other chores. It was a raw effort for the fingers, pulling the hide straight and piercing it with line. As soon as it began to take shape the garment became heavy to hold and stitch. My hands ached by the end of each sitting.

If my family thought it a curious or silly occupation, they did not reveal it. They knew Magda was dear to me and ailing, so they paid me the courtesy of space to sew and hang the item. Sometimes Jonah watched me working through the window, with the look on his face of a man wistful for some previous vision beheld. One morning he knocked on the glass and I opened the window. He held a piece of polished horn up between his fingers, then passed it to me. He tapped his chest, pointed at the cape, and left to join our father in the paddock. I looked at the pretty little object he had made. There was a figure carved into the white tusk button, but I could not descry it. A sitting dog, perhaps. Or a woman's face in cameo.

The winter took hold. There were record snowfalls. The villages were blocked and paraffin ran low. Sugar was rationed at the store. And there was worse to come, the sky-watchers said. The cottage was bitter in the mornings before the range was up, and I put on extra woollens and stamped my feet as I sewed. I felt neither truly myself nor like any other person during this time, I was simply given to the occupation. If I ran a crooked hem and had to unpick a line then I imagined Magda's brant collarbones. I remembered the lavish berries in the autumn hedgerows and thought of those telltale stains on her petties. With every prick I made I wished Magda well again. I wished it and I traded for it. And when the cotton snapped I grasped the bobbin and quickly tied the thread tight again. Each day I put my face against the soft fur and whispered into its darkness, God keep her.

By Christmas Eve I was finished. I came late to mass from brushing the coat down and inspecting it a final time, with every lamp lit to illuminate the parlour, and I received a disapproving look from the seated congregation. But I did not care. I felt triumphant. And I sang the last carol as merrily as it was meant.

*

Magda was delighted with the cape. She got glistery-eyed when she saw it the next morning and got up from her bed like a miracle-walker.

She said, You hang the moon, Dolly Carter, you hang the moon!

And she kissed my cheek and hugged me to her until I blushed scarlet. She had me put the garment over her shoulders and fasten the horn button, and then she curtsied like a proper dame. She looked like a silky portion of night before me, and I did wonder if I hadn't reached down into some charmed well of pitch, contracting with a rabble of spirits to create the thing. The stole remained a little gamey, and it never looked entirely neat, but Magda wore it all through January and February and commented each time she did so how fine it felt.

As warm as sotter loaf, she said.

We buried her in May. She knew exactly what she wanted to be buried in, and though her father protested, the cape was put around her shoulders, over the white communion dress, which still fitted perfectly after all the years. I attended to her laces and brushed her hair. I gave her spring flowers and a stem of vervain. By then the bones had come so far through her she seemed carved from ivory, like the birds the mason set into her stone.

I thought I would miss her and I did miss her prettiness and her mirth. I did miss her gentle candour. But my dreams were not of Magda. The truth of death is a peculiar thing. For when they leave us the beloved are as if they never were. They vanish from this earth and vanish from the air. What remains are moors and mountains, the solid world upon which we find ourselves, and in which we reign. We are the wolves. We are the lions. After so many nights treading the banks with the dogs and my brothers, intent on some mettlesome purpose I did not truly understand, night after night I dreamed of the river. I dream it now: a river of stolen perfumes, winding its way through our inverse Eden.

Vuotjärvi

She stood on the pontoon and watched him swim out. His head above the lake surface grew smaller and more distant. After a while he turned and looked to the shore. His face was white and featureless. It eclipsed as he turned away again and continued swimming. The water was sorrel-coloured, with ruddy patches where the sun lit its depth. When they'd arrived they had knelt on the wooden structure and examined cupped handfuls, trying to discern what its suspension of particles or dye might be. Peat perhaps. Some kind of mineral. The rich silt of the lake bed. Evergreens lined the edge of the glinting mass. Beyond was a vast Scandinavian sky that had, for the duration of their stay, failed to shed its light completely at night. The humidity had surprised them, this far north. The air was glutinous. The meadow grass and the barks glistened. Locals complained that it was the worst year ever for mosquitoes. Spring conditions had suited the larvae. They were everywhere now, whining in the air, their legs floating long and dusty behind them. In the outhouse there was no escaping. They seemed to rise invisibly from the walls, from the chaff and sawdust covering the silage container below the hole. She had rows of bites along her ankle bones, legs and arms. Each bite was raised into a welt, but was not itchy.

Though there was electricity at the cottage, they had been carrying buckets of the orange water up to wash plates and cups. A natural well was being directed to the house, they had been informed, but the plumbing was not yet complete. Two other cottages were tucked into the strong greenery along the shoreline, painted red, shingled, their plots impeccable. There was a pleasing folk-art look about them. Their inhabitants had not been seen much. Wood smoke curled from the sauna sheds in the early evening. The second night, while they'd been standing at the water's edge observing the start of a vague, ineffectual sunset, two forms had exited the nearest shed, made their way along a scythed path, and entered the lake. She had waved to them. The Finnish neighbours had waved back, then swum round a pine-covered promontory, out of sight. There was a correctness here, a sensual formality, which she liked very much. *You must always take your shoes off inside*, the friend whose cousin had lent the cottage had said to them. *It's a particular thing.* Since arriving they had worn no shoes at all. Nor much clothing. The grass around the cottage had been softened by a rainstorm. She had woken during the first night to the purring of rain on the cottage roof.

Under her feet, against the tambour of pontoon planks, the lake slapped and knocked. He was three hundred yards out or so. She could see that he was swimming breaststroke. His feet and hands barely broke the surface. He did not turn round again and his movements were slow and regular. His head grew smaller. He had decided to swim to an island in the middle of the lake and back again. It was perhaps a mile and a half altogether. He was a strong swimmer and she was not concerned. At home he went a long way up the rivers. She did not want to join him. She liked swimming, but not any great distance. She was happy to float on her back, her head submerged, listening to the somatic echo. Or she would crouch and unfold in the water, crouch and unfold. Or look down at her hands – two moon-white creatures in the rippling copper.

The lake was deep, but it was not cold. They had already rowed out in the little boat belonging to the cottage and dropped anchor and gone in where the shadows were expansive, the bottom no more than a black imagining. The temperature seemed almost indistinguishable from that of her blood, a degree or two cooler. He had held her waist as they kicked their legs, bringing her gently to him. His shoulders under the surface looked stained, tones of surgical disinfectant. His face was wet. There was a taste of iron when they kissed. Suddenly she had become breathless, from exertion, from the eroticism of their bodies drifting together, the memory of that morning's lovemaking, on their sides, discovering the fit of him behind her, that she should lean away slightly and tip her pelvis as if pouring water from it. That feeling of rapture, of flood, like being suspended.

Her fears had begun to coalesce. The lake depth was unknown and the pressure against her limbs was a trick: it felt no greater than in the shallows. Underneath was vestigial territory. Rotting vegetation. Benthic silence. The scale of her body in this place was terribly wrong. Something was reaching up, pulling down. Urgency to get out made her kick away to the boat, haul against the side and scramble over its rim. Once inside she had rested her head on the oarlock, breathing away the panic, amazed by the direness of the impulse. *Are you OK?* he'd called. *Oh God, for some reason I thought I should feel imperilled, and then I did*, she said. *What an idiot. Look at you. Calm as anything in there.* He acted out a frantic drowning, and she laughed.

She had rowed the boat back to the cottage while he lay against the prow and sunbathed, getting used to the rotation of the long thin oars, the lunge and drag. Soon the vessel began to skim through the water, and was easier to steer. They'd beached the boat, pulling it high up into the trees and looping the rope around a trunk, taking the bung out so the hull wouldn't fill if it rained again. Then they'd walked through the meadow to the cottage, through blooms of airborne pollen and ferrying insects, their shoulders sunburnt, hungry, in no rush to eat. The midday sky was an immense shale. When she lifted her arm her skin smelled of the lake, almost sexual, eel-like. All she had been able to think about was having him move behind her again, fractionally, his hand on her hip, until it was too much, or not enough, and he had to turn her against the bed, rest his weight on her, take hold of her neck, her hair, move harder.

A eucalypt scent. Pine resin. Spruce. The reeds behind her rustled. A breeze combed the lake surface, left it smooth for a moment, then came again. The pontoon rose and sank, instinctively, like a diaphragm. The pages of the book he had left next to his sunglasses and camera flickered. She picked it up. It was a speculative text about humanity's chances of extinction within the century. All the ways it might happen. Plague. Bio-terror. Asteroid impact. *Finland is the right place to read a book like this,* he'd joked as he began it on the plane. *They're such great survivalists. There's some kind of seed bank there, just in case we mess everything up. I think that's in Norway,* she had said. They had read dreadful sections out to each other over the last few days. *The twelve-day incubation period for smallpox means it could spread globally before an epidemic is declared, or contained. Aerosolising sarin is the terrorist's main challenge.* Most unpredictable were the colliders, the super-viruses, strangelets. Dark matter.

She rocked up on her toes and strained to see his head, which was now a tiny brown spot, difficult to identify between the onshore waves. He must be two-thirds of the way to the island. Soon she would see him climb the rocky skirt in front of the huddle of trees, and stand upright. Even at this distance, even minute, she would surely see him, once he was out. Her eyesight was good. He was tall. And he was naked. His pale form would contrast with the dark green hub of the island. He would probably rest for a time then set off back. She put the book down, under the camera.

*

He had decided to make the swim after they'd taken a sauna. The sauna hut was traditional in design, beautifully crafted. He'd prepared it, checked the tank, cleared away the old ashes and built a new fire under the stones, as instructed by the cousin. They had waited for the heat to intensify, then lain on the benches in the cedary fug, listening to the interior wood panelling click and creak. The heat was so dense they were immobilised, robbed of energy. They became soaked with perspiration, reaching out to touch each other with extreme effort. Finally, the situation felt forced, the environment unendurable. They bathed in the lake afterwards, and emerged refreshed. Then he said he would try for the island. *I think it'll take about forty-five minutes, or an hour. Photograph me coming back victorious.*

She could no longer see him in the water so she kept her eyes on the spot where she thought he would probably get out. The foliage mossed together the more she looked. Birds circled over the lake. A bird was calling nearby, within the forest, the notes hollow and looping, a song that did not seem diurnal. Now that she could no longer see him it was hard to remain focused. Her mind wandered. She thought about his sounds of arousal, surprise and relief as the soft obstruction yielded, finding a way inside, acute pleasure in those wet recurring motions, the stunned intervals. They were now experts in the act, which was a series of steady, humid acts. He was becoming more vocal. He would speak to her of what he desired. His assertions, his voice, worked her as if she were being touched. The world before and after was incredibly vivid.

The bird in the forest let up. The fluttering in her chest stopped.

She thought about the blue Arabia crockery they had seen in the antique market by the quay in Helsinki. The city's Russian architecture: the Uspenski cathedral with its golden domes and the sentinelled railway station. The quiet Finnish underlay, restraint and elegance, design that would always oppose corruption. Helsinki was attractive, a clean blend of modern and historic. It lacked people. The drive to the cottage had taken six hours, the arboreal view varying only slightly once outside the city. Road signs were impossible. It was a language so unexported the pronunciation could not even be guessed. It sounded similar to and was possibly rooted in the oldest human language, a cross-continental language, she had read. There were sixty thousand lakes.

Theirs was called Vuotjärvi. It was situated between two bigger lakes, towards the dialect of Savo. The GPS unit had led them off the motorway, down minor roads, then along seventeen kilometres of gravel track, past glimmers of water, almost to their destination. The lane to the cottage was overgrown, its entrance easily missed. They had found the place by calling the owner on her mobile phone, hearing her real voice behind the froth of bushes, and walking towards it. Anna Sutela was delighted to meet them and to lend the cottage. It was older than most of the lake cottages. The previous owner had seen a wolf in the garden. She had prepared a salad for their supper and would eat with them before driving back to Kuopio.

He had been gone forty-five minutes, probably more. The lake had a dark tint to its edges, underneath the tree line. There were small white bars at its centre where the wind was freer. Or a current was moving, flows between the two larger lakes. Time had seemed irrelevant, their circadian rhythms were gone, yesterday they had eaten at midnight, but it was now definitely evening. She searched the little island for his intrusive shape. Perhaps he had arrived and was walking its circumference. If he was still swimming there it meant the exercise was not as easy as anticipated. If he was still swimming there he would need more stamina.

The sky and the lake transferred topical yellow patches between each other. Such eerie empty beauty. She began to feel a little uncomfortable. She should have been watching more carefully, consistently. That was really her only duty. She strained her eyes. There was no sign of him. There was no point calling his name, the distance was too great, and the neighbouring Finns might hear and think her disturbance improper. She stepped to the edge of the pontoon, as if those few extra inches might provide enough clarity to locate him. The wooden structure sank slightly and water lapped across her toes. She stepped back, turned, walked off the pontoon and made her way round the little beach above which the boat was moored. She began to unknot the line tied around the tree trunk.

The sensible thing was to row out. Not because she imagined he was in trouble, just in case. He might be struggling. He might have cramp and be treading water, or be floating in the recovery position. Perhaps he was sitting on the island, tired, having underestimated. Or he might already be swimming back to the cottage and she could accompany him, companionably, encourage him if he was flagging, make sure he was really all right and not in any jeopardy. She should have rowed alongside him from the beginning, not because she thought he wouldn't make it, she did think he would make it, but because the boat would be a handy back-up, eroding none of his achievement, simply ensuring the safety of the swim. Why hadn't she gone? Why hadn't she acted more responsibly? She had been too blasé about the whole thing. The possibility of disaster had not really occurred to her, not in a valid way, a way to make her officiously oversee the exercise. Suppose he was in difficulty, now, beyond her field of vision, somewhere in the water.

She tugged at the mooring. He had knotted the rope earlier that day. The knot looked slack but seemed very stiff and loosened out of its synthetic coils and links only a millimetre or two. Her fingers felt too weak for the operation. This was not supposed to be the hard part. The hard part would be moving the boat from its position up the bank where they had dragged it together, down onto the beach and into the lake. She became frustrated and began to yank at both ends of the line, without regard for its undoing. A horrible feeling was trickling into her. A sense that as she fought, uselessly, he was vanishing. *Fucking thing. Come on.* A small, aggravated cry left her. She stopped for a moment and took hold of herself. She looked at the inelaborate shape in her hands. Then she pushed the standing end of the cord through the tuck. The knot released, and the plastic length buzzed as she pulled it loose. She slid the rope from the trunk and threw it into the boat.

The boat was moulded fibreglass rather than wood, but it had still felt heavy when they'd moved it out of the water before. She was uncertain about managing now, alone, even in reverse, with a down-slope. She had not put on shoes. Her shoes were in the porch of the cottage, on the other side of the meadow, too far away and timewasting to retrieve. She tried not to notice how vulnerable her feet felt. She had on a thin cotton shirt, bikini bottoms. She took a breath, leaned against the prow of the boat and pushed. Her feet dug into the ground. Plush earth, twigs and thistles, pebbles where the bank became beach. The vessel resisted, shunted forward a notch or two, then stuck. She pushed again, got traction, gathered momentum. The boat ground across the stony apron of the beach and slid into the water. The first time she had launched a boat. The first stage in a successful rescue, a solo rescue. Already a positive retrospective was forming in her mind. How it might later be told. She felt a source of energy packed within herself. And adrenalin, like a lit taper.

She lifted an oar, steadied it, fitted the metal ball on its underside into the oarlock, then did the same on the other side. She waded the boat out to thigh level, climbed in, took her position on the seat and pulled with her right arm to turn the boat. She remembered the action. Now it was easy. Now it was simply speed, how fast she could row. She turned and looked at the island, imagined her trajectory, began to pull on the oars. The oars, charming and narrow and traditional when they had tested the boat initially, now seemed impractical. She worked her shoulders hard, exaggerating the strokes, improving them. The water was uniform. Though the boat seemed not to be moving locally she was in fact passing new sections of shore, passing the cottage of the neighbouring Finns and noticing, because of the new angle, their electric-green lawn and jetty with bathing steps, passing the promontory, its congestion of trees, its rocks stepping down towards the glistening surface, passing away from the land. Then she was in open water.

She kept pulling hard. Her grip on the oars was firm. Tenderness to her palms, which would mean blisters. She leaned forward, pushed back. She was making good time. It was not very long since she had lost sight of him. The oarlocks rotated. The paddles washed. She pushed away the image of a sallow indistinct form drifting under the surface. She would find him. He would be stranded on the island. He would be pleased to see her. Or, if he was in difficulty in the water, the sight of the boat coming would sustain him; she would arrive and help him in. She would give him her dry shirt to put on. She would kneel in the hull in front of him and hold him. She would tell him that she was in love with him, because she had not yet told him this, though she had wanted to for weeks, though he must see it, mustn't he, whenever she came alive under him, pushing him back so she could see his eyes in that driven, other state, their concentrated pleading look, or when she suffered that peculiar tearful euphoria in climax, with its physical gain, its fear and foreknowledge of loss. *This is all I want. I can't be without it.*

Her strokes became heavier. Her technique was slipping, or she was tired from rowing earlier. It sounded as if the lake was splashing up against the prow more and more. She would have to break, so that she could recover and realign. She slackened the tight grasp of her hands, flexed her fingers. She turned around to look for him again. Inside the boat was a pool of rusty water.

For a moment she did not understand. A leak. There was a leak. *Shit*. How had it gone unnoticed? Had the bottom been punctured when the boat was moved, either up or down the bank? In the centre of the hull was a small black eye. A small black hole. *No*. In the rush to launch she had not fitted the bung. It was still in the small locker by the pontoon. It was her fault that the vessel was not watertight. *Or, most likely, it will be an unforeseen event, manufactured under the auspices of technological advancement, which finishes humanity*. She let go of the oars and shunted forward on the seat. She cast her eyes around the boat. Rope. The little three-pronged anchor. A sponge. There was nothing with which to bail. She could take off her shirt; stuff it into the hole. But she knew that would fail. The cotton would balloon. The twist of fabric would slip out. She was about half a mile into the lake.

Everything was so quiet.

Suddenly she knew how it would all play out. The boat would continue to take on water and would lug down as she tried to row back, its debilitation unstoppable, and then it would submerse. She would make it to the shore, because she could swim well enough, but it would be ugly and ungraceful, it would involve swallowing water and choking because of the desperation. The rescue would be aborted. He would never make it back. Though she would pick her way along the green shoreline to the Finns as quickly as she could, and bang insanely on their door, and beg to use their boat, and listen as they spoke to the emergency services in their pure, impenetrable language, they would not find him or his body. He would be lost. She would be complicit. She would not ever love in this way again.

She heard herself whimpering. The scenery passed out of focus. Her fear was bifurcating; she could feel the fibrous separation in her chest, the intimate tearing, so uncomfortable she could hardly bear it. Then, without any pain, she sealed, and the fear was singular again, for herself only.

She looked out over the water, and thought, just for a second, that she might see him swimming casually along, close enough to come and help her. If he converted his easy breaststroke into a crawl he could get to her before the boat took on too much water. His presence would somehow ameliorate the crisis. Alone, her chances would be worse. She stood up and the boat rocked. A small oblique tide rolled against her ankle, and withdrew. *Where are you? Please*. She scanned the water. The lake was empty. It was full of the night-resistant sky. She sat down and the seiche came again across her feet. The pool settled. It was four or five inches deep. Something else was in it. That colour. And though she felt overwhelmed by the foreign character of this place, by not understanding its substance, the instinct to fight against it was immediate and furious. A desire that tasted bloody in her mouth. She reached for one oar and then the other. She searched the shore and at first could not differentiate between the tiny cottages. Which was it? Which? The first red-roofed one. With the separate outhouse and sauna. And the little beach. And the meadow that had been left wild, where there had once been a wolf. She turned the boat with her right arm, and began to pull heavily in that direction. *In winter*, Anna Sutela had said to them, *there are twenty hours of darkness. The snow reaches the cottage roof. We do not come here.*

Acknowledgements

Thanks to Peter Hobbs, Lee Brackstone and Mary Morris for reading and editing several versions of these stories. Thanks also to David Watkins, Clare Conville, Lisa Baker, Jane Kotapish and Damon Galgut for critical feedback, and to Trevor Horwood and Jem Poster for copy-editing. Thanks to Elizabeth and Anthony Hall, Anna Sutela, Joanna Härmä, Fiona Renkin and Richard Thwaites for help with research. A special thank you to James Garvey.

The Beautiful Indifference is a work of fiction. Characters, events and place names are products of the author's imagination, or, if real, are not portrayed with geographical and historical accuracy.